Winter in Sweetwater County

Book I
Sweetwater County
Series

Ciara Knight

Also by Ciara Knight

The Neumarian Chronicles
Weighted
Pendulum
Balance

www.ciaraknight.com

Winter in Sweetwater County – Sweetwater County Series
Ciara Knight
ISBN-13: 978-1-939081-05-6

This is a work of fiction. Names, characters, places and incidents either are the product of the author's imagination or are used fictitiously. Any resemblance to actual persons, living or dead, events or locales is entirely coincidental.

ACKNOWLEDGMENTS

This novel would not be possible without the endless dedication of so many. A special thank you to: my family for all their love and support, my editor Cora Artz, my cover artist Robin Ludwig, my critique partner Lindi Peterson, my beta readers Ginger DiFrancesco, Karen Wanke, Margaret Taylor and Heather Mitchell, and a special thank you to April Allen for being the virtual glue that holds me together.

CHAPTER ONE

Welcome to Sweetwater County, Tennessee. Population 5,000. Where your heart and home belong.

Lisa Mortan would soon see if the county motto scribbled on their sign was true.

It had been a long drive from New York City. Lisa slowed as she reached the city limits of Creekside, the smallest town just inside the county line, wincing as icy rain began to pelt the windshield. She pushed every button and pulled every lever while keeping one hand on the wheel and one eye on the road. With a huff, she flipped the handle on the right side of the steering column up and the wipers smeared grime and water across the glass. Taking a long steady breath, her lungs filled with the scent of new leather. Thank goodness, Mark's cologne hadn't invaded the interior of the new car, leaving lingering memories and disappointments.

With a shake of her head, she eyed the charming awnings, in a variety of colors, adorning shops lining both sides of the two-lane road. Passing a hardware and interior design store, Lisa then spotted *J and L antiques.* The muscles at the side of her mouth tugged into a smile and her heart warmed. Who knew one sign could provide so much hope?

A silver truck backed out from an angled parking space, slowing her to a stop. As she waited, she watched a family race from the flower shop's covered front stoop to a mom-and-pop restaurant, huddling together before darting to the next store. Would her life look like that someday, if she kept the baby?

Lisa maneuvered into a space and pressed the stop button, cutting the sedan's engine.

Silence.

A sound she'd struggle with, but the ramifications of returning to New York City, and her former fiancé, urged her to keep an open mind.

Staring into the pristine glass windows between swirly writing, nerves fluttered her belly. This was a new start, a chance to have a life and concentrate on what mattered most, or a place to hide out for a few months. Her head spun between right and wrong, but she shook the thoughts away for now. Tucking her purse under her arm, she shoved the car door open and raced across the sidewalk to the storefront.

Clutching her coat around her middle, she thanked the lord it was winter. She wasn't ready to explain her condition to a bunch of strangers. Not that she was big yet, but she swore anyone who looked at her instantly knew the truth.

A bell jingled overhead, announcing her arrival to all in the store. The smell of coffee and cinnamon filled the warm room, reminding her more of a bakery than an old musty antique shop.

"Be right there," the voice she assumed was Judy's called from beyond a partition, on the other side of a large sleigh bed. If Lisa wasn't about to meet her new business partner in person, she would have thrown her purse on the floor, kicked off her shoes, and climbed the wooden step stool, to crawl under the fluffy sage and antique white quilt covering the huge bed.

"Lisa Mortan? Is that you, hon?" A lady shuffled past a polished wood side table and hugged her. "You weren't due until tomorrow. Did you come straight here?"

"Judy Gaylord?" Lisa asked. The woman's embrace could crack the spine of a bear. She definitely contained more strength than most women her age. Heck, with her auburn hair, bright blue eyes, and porcelain skin, she didn't look a day over forty-five. The pictures on Facebook hadn't done her justice.

"Yes, darling." Judy crossed her arms over her slight frame. "Now, why are you here? You should be resting after that drive."

"I wanted to stop in and meet you in person...partner. Also, I figured we'd have a ton of work to do. I see you've already managed to unpack and stage most of the shop."

"We can change anything you like," she offered.

"No. It looks amazing." Lisa smiled. "But you shouldn't have done all this work yourself." Lisa had been concerned the older woman would only be good for pointing out estate sales and other great finds in the region, but it appeared she was worth a lot more to the store than that.

"It was no trouble. I'm not that old, you know. Besides, my son did most of the unpacking and moving. I believe I mentioned him last time we spoke."

Lisa remembered. Judy had spoken often about him and shared photos of the dark haired, blue eyed dream of a human being. She held up her hands. "I didn't mean..."

"No worries, dear. Most women my age are in their dotage, but I tend to stay active. I won't kick off on you any time soon." Judy chuckled. "Come, have some coffee. It'll warm you up."

Lisa's mouth watered at the thought of her heavenly vice coating her scratchy throat with warm, delicious, joy. Then she frowned. "I'd love to, but I think I'll pass."

"Oh? I thought you were a coffee addict who drank all those froufrou drinks at Starbucks all the time."

"Yes, well, I'm trying to give up caffeine." Lisa straightened. It wasn't a lie...technically.

"Oh, I see. Well, good thing I made decaf. My son says I'm irritatingly energetic when I drink caffeine. Come on." Judy straightened a ceramic cat on a bookshelf and headed toward the back of the store and into a kitchen area. "Sit." She waved Lisa toward a chair at a small, glass-topped dining table. A plate of muffins and scones sat temptingly in the middle.

Just as Lisa was sitting down, the bell jingled once more and she shot to her feet again, feeling like an intruder.

"Mother, I brought your laptop back," a masculine

voice called from the front of the store. "Can you try not to download every virus on the internet, please?" Heavy footsteps thudded against the shop's worn wooden floor.

"Ah, speaking of my son..." Judy set down her coffee cup. "Oh, you guys just have to meet. I'll be right back." She wiped her hands on a dishtowel then dropped it on the counter before disappearing from the room. "It's not my fault my laptop keeps getting sick," she hollered.

Lisa snickered, but remained standing. Her stomach growled and she rotated the plate around, analyzing the soft, warm treats in front of her.

"When you receive an email from Elvis, you don't want to click on the attachment. News flash, Elvis is dead." Her son's baritone voice echoed off the room's high ceilings.

"I'm not so sure." Judy shuffled into the kitchen and Lisa stiffened then turned around.

Judy's son towered over the older woman. The thick winter coat he wore couldn't hide his broad shoulders or thin waist. "Hi," he beamed at her. In another life, she would have been interested in those boyish dimples and bright smile, but not now.

"Lisa, this is my son, Eric. Eric, this is Lisa Mortan," Judy said, gesturing between them.

"It's a pleasure." He gripped Lisa's hand in a firm, yet gentle shake. "I've heard a lot about you."

Judy nudged him forward. "Take her coat, Eric."

Lisa stepped back and pulled her coat tight around her. "I'm still a little chilled, but thanks. It's nice to meet you."

"Sit. Both of you," Judy insisted.

"Mmm, I see you made your famous scones and muffins for Ms. Mortan," Eric said.

"Lisa," she corrected.

Eric squeezed around the table and took the seat next to her. "Well, Lisa. I'm glad you're here. Mom only makes these for people she wants to impress, and I'm only her son." His smile drooped into a playful pout, which he turned on Judy.

"Stop, now. You know that's not true," Judy scolded.

She made muffins for me? No one had made any sort of baked goods for her since she was eight. Lisa swallowed down a soft cry that always tried to escape at the memory of her mother. Even today, her chest burned with longing to see her again. But she'd left without a word, so it didn't matter.

If I decide to keep you, I'd never abandon you in the middle of the night. When she realized her hand was rubbing her belly, she quickly clasped her fingers together.

A small plate slid in front of her. "You have to try one of these. People all over Sweetwater County beg for the recipe, but Mom won't part with it. Something about them being special." Eric popped a piece into his mouth and moaned. "Wow, even better than I remember." His silver-blue eyes glistened in the low light.

The smell conquered her will power and she moved a scone to the small plate in front of her.

Breaking off a bite-sized piece, she tossed it into her mouth. A buttery, sweet explosion coated her tongue, and she closed her eyes, savoring every distinct ingredient.

Eric cleared his throat, startling her from the pleasant burst of flavor that had distracted her, and the memories it took her to. He stared at her, no, not at her. His eyes fixed on her wrist and the dark bruise that peeked out from under the cuff of her coat's sleeve.

CHAPTER TWO

E ric's pulse raced at the black and blue mark, shaped like fingers, which Lisa attempted to cover. Clenching his teeth, he averted his gaze. Based on the size of the marks, a man had done it. Was she attacked? A boyfriend? Perhaps that was why she came to Sweetwater, to hide from an abusive husband. He reached out for a muffin, discreetly scanning her left hand. No wedding ring. Not even a tan line.

This was none of his business. Mom had decided to take on this venture, as insane as it was. Starting a business with a woman that she'd never met outside of cyberspace.

His mother had been right about one thing, though. Lisa Mortan was beautiful. Stuffing another muffin into his mouth, he concentrated on the warm, butter-nutty flavor and forced the thought of Lisa and her light floral fragrance from his mind.

"Thanks so much for helping unpack all of our merchandise," Lisa said, her voice soft yet not wimpy or chirpy.

"My pleasure. It's kept Mom busy...which is a good thing. The idle hands of an energetic woman, particularly when it's your mother, are dangerous," he teased.

His mother brought the coffee pot to the table. "Lisa just arrived from New York. Seeing as how she's new in town, perhaps we could all get together for dinner and get to know each other better."

"I need to return to the office." Eric stood and nodded to Lisa, attempting to ignore her full lips, and big bright eyes. She pushed from the table to stand as well and her coat fell open, revealing the longest legs he'd ever seen. The heels she wore only accentuated every inch of them. Straight chestnut colored hair completed the look, shining under the Halogen pot lights he'd installed last week. "It was a pleasure, but I'm afraid I have a client meeting tonight. Don't let Mom work you too hard."

His mother narrowed her eyes with that go-ahead-and-run-away-coward look she'd perfected. Of course, even he had to admit she was right, but it didn't matter. The last thing he wanted was a woman in his life. Not after what happened with his last girlfriend.

"I'll walk you out," his mother offered.

He thought about dissuading her, but she wouldn't listen anyway. With one last glance at the beauty standing in the middle of the kitchen, he bolted, with a promise to bury himself in work and stay away from Lisa Mortan.

"I told you she was beautiful," his mother whispered.

"Cultured, long legs, smart, and don't forget educated. Yes, I've heard it all. A few times. It doesn't matter. I'm not interested," Eric barked. He didn't mean to be rude, but Judy Gaylord needed a firm hand or she'd take over quick.

"I'm just saying." His mother shrugged in a careless gesture.

Eric halted at the front door, clutching the handle. "Don't. I'm not ready. I'm not sure I'll ever be ready."

His mother's small hand rested between his shoulder blades. "It's been almost two years. It's time to let her go."

"No. I-I can't." He turned the knob.

"It wasn't your fault. You need to stop blaming yourself."

"Yes, it was. I ignored the woman I claimed to love, and when she needed me most, I wasn't there."

Judy stepped to his side. "You didn't know about the baby."

"That doesn't matter. What matters is she's dead. The baby's dead. There's nothing else to talk about." Eric shoved the door open. "I have to go." He fled from the shop into the icy downpour, away from his mother's meddling, from Lisa Mortan and her long firm legs, and from the torture of haunting memories.

CHAPTER THREE

Lisa lifted what felt like the fiftieth box of the day and placed it on the dining table. Rubbing her shoulders, she eyed the last three and sighed. Who knew opening a store would be so tough? Even after all the work Judy and her son had done before she arrived, there was still more staging and unpacking to last another few days.

Judy patted Lisa's back on her way to the cash register, where she deposited a decorative vase half-full of glass beads. "Girl, you look tired. Sit, take a load off."

"I'm fine." When Judy gave her a skeptical look, she said, "Seriously. I know not everyone can be as fit as you, but I'm hanging in there."

Judy waved the compliment away with her hand then took a handful of sunflower-topped pens from the drawer and arranged them in the vase. "Oh, shush. We both know you're half my age, and twice the leg height. You ever a model?"

Lisa laughed. "Me? A model? I don't even like having my picture taken." She slid the box cutter across the strip of packing tape and yanked the top of the box open, the ripping and popping sounds echoing how she felt. Her world had been torn apart and here she was in a small town, trying to put the pieces back together.

She glanced at all the beautiful merchandise and realized her dream of having a life outside the craziness of New York City, and all the judgment that went with it, was displayed elegantly around her. Perhaps she could stay here indefinitely and raise the baby, if this store worked out. It didn't have to be a temporary investment, or a detour on her path in life. It could be her home.

Judy donned her coat and slipped her purse over her arm. "Going to collect a few items from the Mitchell's. I'll be back in an hour. Now, you leave whatever heavy lifting there is for Eric. He'll be around on his lunch break. Feel free to take a break when he gets here," Judy said, and Lisa could have sworn the older woman winked.

"I'm sure I can manage. I hate to keep bothering him. Besides, Judy, I think we need to talk." Lisa tagged and placed eight linen napkins on the antique wooden top of a formal dining table, stalling to find the right words. "I get the impression you hope Eric and I will be...well, more than just friends. Trust me, you don't want that."

Judy retrieved her lipstick from her purse and smoothed burgundy across her mouth. "Oh, dear, don't be silly. Besides, don't worry about bothering him. He needs the distraction. And those legs are definitely a distraction." She capped the lipstick and slipped it back into her purse.

"No, please don't go there. Besides, he wouldn't be

interested." Lisa didn't want this endeavor to go belly up before they even started. She'd sunk all her savings, everything, into this in an attempt to flee New York, and Mark. Setting her only son up with an unwed mother would never go over well. Especially in a small town like Creekside—as, the internet put it, the *sleepy little town in the heart of the Bible belt.* The one place Mark was sure never to visit. He'd turned his back on God the day his father committed suicide, and would never set foot in a town like this.

"Why not? You're tall, green eyed, and have the silken chocolate brown mane of a prize pony." Judy waved her hand once more then hurried to the door. "What guy wouldn't want you?" She disappeared before Lisa could even open her mouth to reply.

She stared after the older woman, her mouth and throat gone dry. *Only the father of my child.* She knew she had to tell Judy soon. Maybe if they could get through the opening, and let a few weeks go by then... Judy would know her better and not want to run away screaming. Then she could help Lisa find the perfect parents to raise her baby before she returned to New York. If there were good parents anywhere, they had to be in this town.

The door clicked shut, giving Lisa the excuse to keep her secret a little longer. She rubbed her belly and sat in the chair by the side table, pushing another small box around with her toe.

All of this was so insane. Perhaps Mark was right. Maybe she had no business having a baby. *Perhaps I should have an...* Her stomach rolled at the thought.

No. *I couldn't do it.* Even if she had the baby and gave it up for adoption, it was better than terminating. "I can't just get rid of you like an out of season shoe. No matter how much Mark protested—" She swallowed. "—and threatened." Her hand slipped from her belly to her wrist, the bruise only a pale yellow now.

The door jingled and Eric stepped inside.

She quickly pulled her sleeve down and poofed out her loose shirt.

He rotated his broad shoulders, removing his coat one arm at a time. "Where's Mom?"

"She ran out to pick up a few more things. Grand opening's tomorrow." Lisa clutched the corner of the box and lifted it from the ground. Dozens of envelopes slipped out and spread across the floor as the bottom of the box broke. She tossed the box to the side and bent down to pick them up. On hands and knees, she swiped them into a pile and raked them into her blousy shirt.

"Here's another one." Eric retrieved a small, antiqued looking envelope and flipped it over. "This is addressed to Mom. Its post marked in the late sixties."

She pushed up and sat back down on the dining chair. "Who's it from?"

"Don't know." He scrubbed his chin. "Can't make it out. Hand me another one."

She flipped through the ones she'd scooped into her shirt. "Here. This one says PFC Benjamin."

His fingers grazed hers and a shock bolted up her hands. Crazy pregnancy hormones were making her super sensitive. But this time, she wouldn't let them trick her into falling for the wrong guy. It never worked out. Relationships never lasted. Besides, she was pregnant. What guy would want to take on a woman about to have a baby?

"It's from before my parents were married. But...she never mentioned anyone from the military." His brows furrowed as he slid his finger under the flap.

"You can't read them. Not without her permission." She held her shirt tight to her and sauntered to the counter, unloading them near the cash register. "If she wants to share, she will. Now, hand it over." She held out her hand and gave the sternest look she could manage.

He lifted his gaze from the envelope to her outstretched palm then to her eyes. His dark pupils widened until the sky blue pools she thought she could lose herself in were nearly covered. He stepped forward, his cologne tugging at her determination. Not the urban, yuppie scent her olfactory senses were used to, but a manly, rich aroma of spice and musk.

His lips tugged at one corner. Breath lodged in her throat as he leaned in, resting his elbow atop the counter. He waved the envelope in front of her. "Only until I can find out her secret."

She snatched it and returned it to the rest of the correspondences.

"So, do *you* have a secret?" he asked. He straightened to his full height, shoulders back, but not in the intimidating way Mark would stand. There was no real threat, just an air of prodding where she didn't want him to.

"No. Don't be ridiculous," she said, turning on her

heels and heading back to the boxes. Anything to escape the cologne teasing her interest in something she could never have.

He leaned his hip against the counter and crossed his arms over his broad chest. "You enter into a business with my mom, who you have no prior relationship with, move to a small town, and invest in a building and supplies unseen. So, which is it? Are you running away from something, or looking for something?"

Her heart slammed into her sternum. *Oh God, does he know?* But how? Certainly she had more time before she faced everyone. She hadn't even convinced herself she'd made the right decision. How in the world would she convince everyone else?

"I know," Eric continued casually. "You're an outlaw, running from some horrific crime you committed back in New York City. You worked at a museum, right? So, you're an art thief then." He smiled, bearing bright, straight teeth before he leaned over the counter and gently tugged her hand until the yellow bruise on her wrist peeked from under her sleeve. "My guess is you're running from something, or someone."

She snatched her arm away. A wave of heat seared through, erupting a thundering pulse in her ears. Too personal, too fast. She needed to turn the conversation around before his compassionate eyes drew the truth from her lips. This man before her looked like a God, had a saint for a mother, and surrounded her with the feeling of safety. But it was a farce, an image her *prego* brain had invented due to feelings of loneliness and abandonment. She didn't need a shrink to tell her that. Her knees weakened and she perched on the side of the table to keep from falling to the ground.

"Whatever you're here for, we'll keep you safe." His voice deepened with a promise of protection.

Yep, crazy prego brain.

She gave him a weak smile. "You caught me. You going to turn me over to the art thief police? That painting over there isn't really from an old attic. It's a Rembrandt."

His deep laughter filled the room and a twinkle appeared in his eyes she hadn't noticed before.

"I like that," she mumbled.

"What?" he asked.

"Your laugh. It's one of those laughs that can make a bad day turn good."

His face immediately morphed from the carefree look of a young man bantering with a friend to the wounded look of someone broken. A suspicious twitch quirked his lips, raising his cheek close to his eye. "Where did you hear that?" he asked, backing away. His mouth pressed in a firm line and a sadness tugged at his brows.

"What? Uh, nowhere." Her eyes followed him as he rushed to the door. *What did I say?* "Where are you going? You're mother said you'd help with the heavy lifting."

"Mom took this too far. It's one thing to introduce us, but it's another to..." He shoved his arms into the pockets of his coat then turned to face her. "You know

17

what? You're right."

"About what?"

"I shouldn't read Mom's letters. They're private and people shouldn't meddle into private affairs." Without another word, he bolted from the store, leaving only the chill of the winter air behind.

CHAPTER FOUR

Lisa retrieved a bottle of water from the fridge in the kitchen. Twisting the top off, she leaned against the wall, searching for an answer to what just happened. One minute he was laughing, and the next he looked like she'd stabbed him. What had she said?

The jingle of the door's bell drew Lisa through the swinging door to the front of the store.

"Wow. What was that about?" A woman with crazy blonde, curly hair entered with Judy.

Judy kicked the door closed behind them with a slam. "It wasn't you."

"Is he still hung up on—"

"Everyone can have a bad day," Judy said. "Put that over there." She tilted her head to the corner of the room then set an opened box full of candlesticks and clocks on the dining table. "Cathy Mitchell, this is Lisa Mortan."

Cathy approached Lisa with a gloved hand outstretched, her curly locks bouncing high around her head. "Pleasure, darling."

"Nice to meet you," Lisa replied.

"Why you don't have an accent at all. I was

expectin' some curt city girl with a northern accent." Cathy tried to turn her southern drawl into a Jersey clip, but it sounded more like a false twang from a bad movie.

"I'm originally from out west." Lisa eyed the intricately carved wood and etched glass candlesticks in the box. "These are beautiful."

"My great-grandmama's," Cathy beamed.

"You want to part with these?" Lisa traced the heart design on the side of one of the candlesticks. Why would anyone want to give away a family heirloom? Certainly, the emotional attachment was worth more than what the store could bring. If she had inherited anything from family members, she'd never part with it.

"I wanted to do my part to help launch a new local business. It's always important to support your neighbors."

Lisa caught Judy rolling her eyes behind Cathy's back, indicating the purpose wasn't entirely selfless. "Well, we thank you. Of course, we'll barter for a great price," Lisa replied. Cathy's lips drooped. Judy cupped her mouth to keep from laughing aloud. *What did I say this time?*

"Yes, well. I don't need the money, it's just good charity," Cathy said.

Judy dropped her arms down to her sides. "That's so generous of you. Thank you so much."

Cathy turned to Judy then back to Lisa, her brows arched high above her eyes, yet her forehead didn't move. "Yes, well, I..." Cathy straightened her coat and cleared her throat, "I hope it works out. I don't like to gossip, but I thought you should know. The Russells are talking about opening their own store. You know, she can't handle anyone else having success without them involving her. You better watch your back, Judy. Did you hear about her smokin'—"

Judy held up her palm. "I appreciate your warning. It's good of you to have our back. I know you don't like to gossip and you're extremely busy."

"Busy?" Cathy's eyes lit with recognition, as though she'd just remembered something important. "Oh darling, you know I'm running the Sweetwater County Hoe Down tonight. I've been organizing the silent auction, calling people, not to mention tagging all the items." Cathy rubbed her temples with exaggerated circles.

"We should let you get back to it," Lisa offered, anxious for the woman to be on her way. "Thank you so much for donating this to the shop. If you find anything you like here, we'd be happy to give you a discount," Lisa added, attempting to help Judy, who obviously also wanted to get away from Cathy.

Judy mouthed *thank you* and shuffled to the door.

"Well, I don't buy used items, but if you ever have anything new, let me know. I'll see you tonight, right?" Cathy asked. "We all have to do our part to help the less fortunate on the other side of the creek." She whirled like a beast, her hair a tarnished halo around her head, then marched out the door. *Bang.* The ceramic cat resting on the side table waffled and fell to the floor, landing on an oriental rug with a thud.

"Well, there wouldn't be a proper Sweetwater County store opening without Cathy Mitchell." Judy clapped her hands together. "Okay, what's left?"

"Nothing really." Lisa gestured around the room. "There's just one small box and a few pieces of furniture. Oh, and we found some letters. They're up on the counter."

"Letters?" Judy asked.

"Yes. When I lifted that box, they fell through the bottom. I believe they were written back in the sixties and early seventies."

The color in Judy's face drained and she wobbled before resting on the sage and antique quilt on the bed. "I forgot about those." She shook her head. "Did Eric read them? Is that why he stormed out of here?"

"No. I wouldn't let him. They belong to you. But...I'm not sure what happened. He was laughing about something, and I complemented him then he just...bolted."

"That's strange." Judy rose from the bed, her eyes distant, and ambled to the counter.

"I said something about how his laugh could turn a bad day good, but I don't know why that..."

Judy stopped in her tracks and silence filled the room. Two long breaths later, she continued forward with a slight chuckle. "It's nothing you did, dear. Everyone has their skeletons to deal with. My son's no different."

Lisa wanted to ask what that meant, but that box wasn't one she intended to unpack just yet. If she pried into their personal lives, there was a good chance they'd pry into hers. "So, who are the letters from, if I may ask?"

"From a long lost love," she mumbled, lifting each letter one by one.

Lisa knew she should shut her mouth and let Judy be, but she was curious. "Did you know him before marrying Eric's dad?"

"Yes. He was his cousin." Judy opened one envelope, a glint of tears in her eyes. "He was the love of my life."

"What happened?" Lisa asked tentatively.

Judy rested the opened letter on the counter and looked off into some other world. "He was captured during the war and presumed dead."

"I'm so sorry." Lisa's voice broke for the sorrow her new friend must have felt.

"Yes, well, it was a long time ago." Judy folded the letter and returned it to the envelope unread. "We've all loved and lost. I'm sure you have, too."

"Yes." Lisa averted her gaze and concentrated on not rubbing her belly.

Judy came around the counter. "I think it's time for us to have a sit-down. We might have just met in person a few days ago, but we've been chatting online for months. Even so, there are a few things we should flush out." Judy donned an apron, smoothing the wrinkles from the front. "I'll go make some decaf tea and, I tell you what, I'll share my story, if you tell me yours. Not all the deep dark secrets, but the overall picture. When you're ready to share the rest, I'm sure you will. As will I."

Lisa's throat went dry. What did Judy want to know? How much did she have to share? Lisa paced the store nervously while Judy busied herself in the kitchen, and her eye caught sight of the curtains hanging from the far wall. The set she'd ordered for the New York condo. The ones that arrived the day she told Mark she was pregnant. The day he said he'd kill her if she didn't have an abortion.

CHAPTER FIVE

Eric turned onto Main Street, heading for his office and his chest tightened at the memory of Mary Lynn by his side all through high school. This small town was filled with memories of her—the two of them strolling down the sidewalk, hand in hand, or eating sundaes at the ice cream parlor he'd just passed. She'd make funny faces as they shared fries at the local diner across the street, telling him how his laugh turned her grey day bright.

Mother. How much had she told Lisa?

Pulling into his parking place, he cut the engine and clenched the steering wheel. He'd finally found a daily routine that didn't involve constant visions of holding Mary Lynn dying in his arms, and nightmares of him abandoning his own baby.

Tap. Tap.

Eric turned to the driver's side window to see a young girl stepping back from his car. He unclenched his hands and morphed into Eric Gaylord, attorney at law, a look he'd perfected while working in New York. With his briefcase in tow, he opened the door. "Can I help you?"

"Yes, sir. You're Attorney Gaylord, correct?" Her light eyes darted back and forth, scanning the street behind him. "I was hoping I could speak with you before heading back to school."

She looked familiar, but even in a small town, there were still some he didn't know, or hadn't met since he'd returned a year ago. "Certainly, Ms.—"

"Burton, Rose Burton."

Eric hit the lock button on his remote and the doors all clicked in unison. "As in Burton Enterprises?"

The girl glanced left and right, as if the world was listening in to their conversation. "Yes, that's the one." She pulled her purple coat sleeves over her knuckles and danced between feet. She was obviously plagued with distress. He'd been around enough corporate people to know how challenging that kind of life could be. Perhaps she just needed to speak to someone.

Part of him wanted to tell her that she needed to return with her parents, but the other part wanted to help her. What if she was in trouble and her parents were part of the issue? "Would you like to come to my office?" Eric asked.

"No. That's why I came to your car. Your secretary knows my mom. They're in the same tennis league or something. I have some money saved, but...I'm not sure if it's enough to have you retained. That's what it's called right?"

Eric smiled and nodded. "Yes, there's usually a retainer fee."

"How much?" Rose asked eagerly.

Eric analyzed her face and hands, but didn't see

any signs of bruising. His mind couldn't help but instantly assume the worst before exploring other options, not when he'd grown up watching someone being battered on a regular basis.

Mary Lynn always had bruises during high school. Of course, the first year they dated, she had him convinced it was from cheerleading.

Perhaps it was something small that this girl thought she needed an attorney for, but likely all she needed was advice. "Why don't you tell me what this is about, and then we'll figure out if I can help you."

Ms. Burton toyed with her bottom lip and lowered her chin, avoiding eye contact. "I want to divorce my parents."

Eric fought the desire to chuckle. This young girl obviously had a disagreement about something and now thought she could leave her parents. It wasn't the first time he'd been asked that.

She lifted her chin and straightened, her face serious. "I want to sue for emancipation."

Eric's amusement died, his heart aching at the sadness in the girl's wide eyes. Something beyond a disagreement had brought this on, at least in her mind. "I'd need more details." *Don't get involved in this. It's Burton Enterprises.* "If there is abuse in your home, I encourage you to report it to the authorities."

"No. They don't beat me." She rolled her eyes.

"Is it a disagreement? Perhaps you can seek family counseling—"

"No," Ms. Burton snipped.

"Mr. Gaylord, I have an urgent call for you,"

Connie, his secretary called out to the parking lot from the front door of his office building.

"I'm going to need more details prior to taking your case. Here." Eric pulled a card from his briefcase and a pen. "I'll give you my direct line. We can set up an appointment for you on a morning my receptionist is out of the office."

"Thank you." Ms. Burton took the card. "I appreciate it so much."

Eric shook his head. "I'm not saying I'll represent you. I'm saying I'm willing to hear more about your case."

The young girl reached for her purse. "I only have—"

"No need to worry about money right now. Let me hear more before we decide on any financial obligations."

"Okay. Thanks. I better get back to school. Lunch period's almost over." She turned, her expensive glittery bag catching his eye.

What was he thinking? Taking on a case with the daughter of the biggest business owner in all of Sweetwater County, and four other counties to the west, didn't seem like a good idea.

He slid his phone from his pocket and headed for the door Connie was still holding open.

"Who was that child?" Connie asked.

"Some teenager asking for legal advice." Eric opened his text messages and selected his mother.

"She looks familiar," Connie mumbled under her breath.

He chose to ignore her and continue passed her desk and into his office. "If my mother calls, please put her through." He dropped his briefcase on his desk and typed, *We need to talk* then hit *send*. "Connie, do you mind running out and getting us some coffee?" Eric called out.

"Sure, but it's afternoon, you know. You'll be up all night," his secretary protested.

"Yes, well, I have enough work to keep me up all night, so that's not a problem."

"If that's what you want, but you know you'll be cranky in the morning," Connie mumbled as she left the office.

Once he heard Connie's car start, he opened his top left drawer and removed the small box he kept there. Opening it, he retrieved the picture of Mary Lynn. The one they'd taken in Rockefeller center at Christmas, before the fight.

Her cheeks were red from the cold wind, and her brownish-red hair was cropped short. She was snuggled into his side and smiling, while he only sat with a blank stare. She'd dragged him out there, saying she wanted to see the sights and give him a special Christmas present. After an hour of her begging, he put aside his work and took her sightseeing, but all he could do was think about a big corporate meeting he had to prepare for the day after Christmas. He hadn't even given her his undivided attention on Christmas Eve.

Guilt hammered away at his soul. He dropped his head into his hand, accidentally bumping the still open drawer, and something jingled. Glancing down, he spotted the Christmas present Mary Lynn had wanted to give him so bad but never had the chance. The one he'd found at his apartment after the next morning. He choked on gut-wrenching grief.

The silver baby rattle.

CHAPTER SIX

The teapot squealed in warning that Judy would be returning soon and Lisa still hadn't figured out what she would share. Perhaps she could keep Judy focused on her long lost love from before she was married. It sounded intriguing.

Though their grand opening was the following day, the front door remained unlocked. Customers had come in a few times, asking about the opening, so there was a good chance their conversation could be cut short. Or better yet, she could just tell Judy she was on an adventure. Tired of city life and trying something new. Yes, that was it.

"Here you go, dear." Judy carried two cups and saucers to the antique wood table near the cash register. "Mint tea, no cream or sugar. Just the way you like it."

Funny how Judy already knew that about her. Mark didn't even remember she liked coffee and tea, despite her daily habit. And when he had remembered, he would belittle her for it, saying it stained her teeth. Looking back now, there were signs. Many signs that their relationship wasn't really what she thought it was.

So, why hadn't she seen them earlier?

"Tell me about your mysterious pen pal," Lisa gushed, not wanting to give Judy an opportunity to pry into her past.

"He was my first and forever love." Judy sat across the dining table, moving merchandise that had yet to be displayed out of the way. "Don't get me wrong. I loved Eric's father, but it was different. A comfy, protected, happy to have a good man kind of love. But I loved James in an I'd-die-for-you kind of way." She sipped her tea and smacked her lips. "We planned on marrying when he returned from Vietnam. Heck, we'd planned on marrying before he'd even left, but I was too young. We had to wait, promising when he was due home for leave after his tour, we'd be married." Her voice softened. "But that wasn't to be."

"I'm so sorry." Lisa reached out and cupped Judy's soft hand. "That war cost so many so much."

"You were affected, too?" Judy released Lisa's hand and returned to her tea.

"Yes. My dad returned from the war with Post Traumatic Stress Disorder and a drug problem. Instead of my mother helping him, trying to lift him up, she bolted."

"You were left behind with a sick father?" Judy asked.

Lisa nodded. "I took care of him until he died. It wasn't so bad. On good days, he was the best father around. Other times..." Lisa hadn't thought about him for almost a year. She'd laid the pain to rest the day she buried him. "So, James never made it home?" she asked, redirecting the conversation.

"I received word a month prior to our wedding date that he was missing in action. The day we were supposed to be married, we got the news. He'd been captured and presumed dead."

Lisa gasped. "Oh, Judy."

"It was long ago. I was lucky. I'd been loved like no other woman on Earth. James had eyes for me and only me. He showered me with affection. He was a good man." Judy shook her head softly then her sad eyes turned bright. "Now, your turn."

Lisa clutched her teacup and took a long sip.

"Come on, now," Judy urged. "If we're gonna work together and become best friends, you need to start talking." The older woman sat across from her with determined narrowed eyes.

"There isn't anything to tell."

"Bull hockey." Judy leaned back and crossed her arms over her chest. "Spill it, young lady. I know why I signed on for this little project. I'm an old lady with nothing to do. I wanted an adventure, a change of pace. And I wanted a partner. I'll admit you being a young woman from beyond Sweetwater County wasn't a bad point either. My son doesn't belong with any of these women. He's too cultured and refined, but he refuses to leave me here alone since his dad died." Judy bit her bottom lip and arched a brow while Lisa fiddled with the tag hanging over the side of her teacup. "Okay, I'll guess," Judy said finally. "You lost your job and boyfriend and needed a change."

"That's somewhat true," Lisa answered, hoping the

discussion would stop there. "He was my fiancé, not my boyfriend, and I quit my job since he pretty much owned the people at the museum with his *donations*."

"New York City is an awful big place. Plus there're tons of museums. What brought you to our small town?"

"I wanted to leave the city, settle into a quieter way of life."

"Oh, honey, this town ain't quiet. Gossip is an epidemic here. Everyone knows everything about everyone, whether you live east or west of the creek. And that's not just a geographical feature around here. That creek's an epic divide of social class and economic situations." Judy relaxed in her chair, her face softening, and she leaned over her cup of tea. "Does it have anything to do with the bruise on your arm? Are you running away from an abusive man?"

It was then that Lisa realized she'd been tugging at her sleeve. She let go and shook her head. "It wasn't like that. He never hit me or did anything to hurt me in the past. We just had a disagreement. He didn't want me to leave, so he grabbed my arm and wouldn't let go."

"Did he threaten you?" Judy nudged.

Lisa thought back to that night. The cold rain, candlelight, the hours she'd spent preparing to tell him she was pregnant. Never had she imagined he would have taken it the way he did. The hatred in his eyes and the accusations that she was trying to trap him and ruin his life bombarded her once more. "Yes, but it was in the heat of the moment. I don't think he'd actually hurt me."

"Perhaps not, but does he know where you went?" Judy asked.

"Please don't worry. I told him what he needed to hear. He won't be looking for me," Lisa reassured her. As long as Mark thought the pregnancy was terminated, he'd leave her alone and there was no way he'd find out otherwise.

"And what did you fight about?" Judy lifted the teacup to her lips.

"Nothing really. It doesn't matter now. I saw him for the man he is and I left. Simple as that." Lisa straightened. She'd never agree to stay in a relationship where a man hurt or threatened her. Mark had never even raised his voice until that night.

"Good for you, dear." Judy gave her a smile. "Okay, you keep your secret, and I'll keep the rest of mine. Someday maybe we'll both be ready to share." She pushed from the table. "It's late so let's finish up. I need to run an errand, but I'll meet you back here and we can go to the Hoe Down together."

Lisa thought of all her own boxes that needed unpacking at the house she was renting, but it could wait. The event would be a great place to meet people from town. Perhaps even a nice couple who would adopt her child.

Judy clicked off a side table lamp. "I can't believe the opening's tomorrow. Oh, and you'll be coming to my house after we close to celebrate. No excuses."

"That would be great." Lisa cleared the table, wondering if Eric would be there. "If I said something wrong to Eric, please extend my apologies."

Judy smiled. "Don't worry about it, dear. He'll be there tonight. You can talk to him then. But remember, we all have our secrets. Eric is no different."

CHAPTER SEVEN

Eric was buried in paperwork when he heard two light taps on his office door. "Yes?" he asked, not bothering to look up.

The door squeaked and Connie stuck her curly brunette head through the opening, her perfectly manicured fingers grasping the edge of the door. "Your mom's here to see you," she said.

He'd been waiting all day to give her a piece of his mind. But lucky for her, it had been a long one, with enough time to cool off. Having already decided to be blunt and honest, with none of his mother's games, he leaned back in his chair. "Show her in and then you can call it an early evening. I know you'd like to go to the social tonight."

"Won't you be there?" Connie quirked an eyebrow. "There'll be a lot of broken hearts if you don't show."

"I'm not really in the mood for a party, but feel free to have a drink of the infamous Sweetwater punch for me."

She smiled, something of a rarity around the office. "Well, I hope you change your mind. Good evening."

"Good night, Connie."

"Oh, he'll be going." His mother's voice sparked his resentment for her meddling, but he leaned forward and rested his elbows on the desk. He'd treat this like he did his client meetings, particularly when their families were present, with logic and a clear mind.

"There you are." His mother stepped into his office, but remained in the doorway. "You said you wanted to see me, so here I am."

"Yes, I did." He held out a hand to direct her to the seat in front of him.

"Really?" She arched a brow at him. His mother took the chair and yanked it around the desk so they were sitting side by side. His attorney façade chipped a little at his mother's concerned eyes. "What's going on, son?" she asked, leaning forward to offer him a hand in comfort, but he leaned back and narrowed his eyes.

"I want to be direct and to the point."

"I'd expect no less," his mother replied.

He cleared his throat and readied for a good Gaylord argument. "You had no right to tell Lisa about Mary Lynn."

"You're right. I don't."

Eric paused, narrowing his eyes at her. "I don't understand. Is that your apology?"

"No. I have nothing to apologize for. Lisa told me what happened, and I had nothing to do with it. Now I have one question for you."

"What?"

His mother crossed her arms over her chest. "Have you ever considered that you have a laugh that makes more than just one girl's heart melt? Maybe that's why two different women told you basically the same thing. Or do you just like to accuse your mother of being the town busy body, with nothing better to do but gossip about her only son?"

He shrank back in his chair, feeling like that twelve-year-old boy who got caught with his mom's Victoria Secret catalog. "No."

"Well, maybe you should." His mother remained straight, with her don't-cross-me-son pinched brow.

"Fine, let's say you didn't tell her—"

"I didn't."

Eric sighed. "Then let's focus on the fact that you brought Ms. Mortan here intentionally, so that I'd be interested in dating her."

"Boy, aren't you egocentric? How about we focus on the fact that I wanted something to occupy my time since your father passed? Perhaps giving up working all those years to make sure my son was healthy and happy and waiting until he was grown and gone before I pursued my dream is something I should apologize for. Do I think you two could be great together? Yes, I do, but you're too stubborn to see it, so if you miss out on a good thing, then that's on you, not me."

"Then you do admit to wanting to set us up," Eric retorted.

"Yes, but I didn't think I needed to hit you over the head with one of those heavy law books on your shelf to get you to notice her, though."

"I noticed her all right," he grumbled.

"Then what's the problem?" his mother asked.

He clutched the armrests. "You know what the

problem is."

"No. I don't. You lost someone who you cared about deeply and now you're wasting your life living in the past," she scolded.

"That's what I deserve." Eric shot up from the chair and paced the room. "It's my fault Mary Lynn and my own baby are dead." Remorse clutched his heart and squeezed it until he thought it would explode inside his chest.

"No, it's not your fault," his mother whispered from behind him.

"Isn't it? She came to me in New York, to tell me we were having a baby and what did I do? I sent her away. She died because I was too busy to spend any time with her."

"That's not what happened." His mother's steps sounded behind him, and her warm hand pressed to his back. "Son, you've tortured yourself for far too long, to the point you believe your own guilt. She tried to trap you into marrying her because she knew she was losing you. You fell in love as children, but then you grew up. Heck, you even wanted to break it off with her in high school, but each time you tried, her father would beat her, or she'd end up in some sort of crazy mess. Don't get me wrong, Mary Lynn was a lovely girl and she wanted the best for you, as long as it included her. You didn't send her away. She went off in hysterics, before she even told you about the baby, and there was nothing you could do to stop her."

His hands shook at the memory of their last fight. He'd told her it wasn't going to work out. That he loved her, but they were too different. "If I would have known about the baby..."

"I have no doubt you would have married her and been the best father and husband you could have been."

"I don't know." Eric fought the lump in his throat. He'd only cried twice since the accident, when she died in his arms and when the doctor told him his child was dead."

He heard a drawer slide open then a jingle sounded behind him. "I do. You were born to be a father. I know you'll be an excellent one, but by holding onto something tragic, punishing yourself with undeserved guilt, you're not giving love another chance."

"I don't know if I can," he said, his voice gruff with emotion.

"I do." She handed the rattle to him and he clutched it in his palm. "It's time to let go of the guilt and embrace what's in front of you before it's gone. I know you like her."

"I just met her," Eric protested.

"Yes, but you look at her in a way you never did with Mary Lynn. Trust me. You need to let go before it's too late and you lose out on something amazing." She squeezed his hand briefly then turned and left the office without another word.

He stumbled back to his chair and held tight to the small silver object that meant so much. "I don't know if I can," he whispered.

CHAPTER EIGHT

The country music blared from inside the large barn-like structure ahead. Judy patted Lisa's back. "Don't worry, dear. I don't think Eric will be anything but kind."

"It's not that." Lisa shook her head and took a deep breath.

"What is it then? You look like you've been in another world since we left the shop."

"Oh, it's nothing. I've just been thinking about where my life has been and where it's going, that's all."

"As long as that's all." Judy laughed. "It's a party, darling. Your troubles will still be there when it's over. Come on, let's boogie."

Lisa chuckled. "Boogie?"

"Crumping?" Judy offered instead with a smile.

Lisa laughed so hard she could barely climb the three steps to the open doors.

Eric snuck up, slid between them, and wrapped his arms around their shoulders. "What's so funny?"

"Your mom wants to crump."

"Great, I'm having flashbacks of my sixth grade dance with Janie Walker." Eric shook his head.

"What?" Judy asked indignantly. "I was the star of that show." She flung her hair back and lifted her chin like a diva, sending both Eric and Lisa into hysterics.

Entering the oversized building, Lisa realized it wasn't a barn at all, but a huge community center dressed up like a barn.

The music stopped and Cathy Mitchell took the stage. "Welcome, everyone. As you know, this event is to raise money for those less fortunate kids, so dig deep into your pockets and leave with some great stuff. We've got gift certificates for the diner, barber shop, and the new J and L Antique Store opening tomorrow." Cathy winked at Judy before continuing her spiel. "There are gift baskets and..."

Lisa scanned the room, noticing all the townspeople dressed in overalls and big frilly skirts. She leaned into Eric and whispered, "Where are the kids?"

"What do you mean?" Eric asked.

"Shouldn't the kids be here if this party is for them?"

Eric slipped his hand from her shoulder to her lower back. Releasing Judy, he turned and tilted his head to the side. "You know, I've asked that same question."

"Then what's the answer?"

Eric leaned over, cupping the back of her head so he could whisper in her ear. Her neck tingled at his touch. "That I was crazy for suggesting such a thing." His warm breath kissed her ear, and everything else around her faded from her attention.

When he released her and stepped back, she regrouped quickly. "It doesn't seem right. Next time, we should bus the kids in ourselves." She could just imagine how much fun kids would have in the large open space, with hay bales to climb on and hide behind.

Eric smiled one of those winning, brighten-your-day kind of smiles.

"...so place your bids and enjoy the party," Cathy finally concluded her speech and the music vibrated the wooden floor beneath Lisa's feet once more. Cathy left the stage and whirled around the room, ordering people to complete various tasks.

Lisa stood on her tiptoes. "I...I'm sorry for whatever I said that upset you," she offered her apology, battling the music to be heard.

"No, it wasn't you. I thought Mom had meddled where she didn't belong, but I guess it was just a coincidence."

Judy maneuvered close to them and shouted, "Eric." She squeezed his hand and Lisa was sure their eyes had a chat without a word leaving their lips. Judy smiled, he nodded. "You mind hanging with Lisa for a bit and introducing her around? I need to speak to Cathy about something."

"Sure, my pleasure." Eric slid his hand into Lisa's and guided her to the refreshment table. "You should try the punch. It's one of those infamous Sweetwater recipes."

Lisa took the plastic cup he offered and sipped the pale red liquid. A strong, bitter tasting beverage slid down her throat. Coughing, she set the cup back on the table. "What's in that? I haven't tasted anything like that since college."

Eric chuckled. "Sweetwater Punch. You do know where the name Sweetwater came from, right?"

Lisa still struggled against the sting in her throat as she said, "It's named after the creek."

"Yes, but do you know why it's called Sweetwater Creek?" Eric's dimples made an appearance, soothing her scorched throat. "Back in the day, Sweetwater was code for Whiskey. This county was the hub for supplying New York City with libations during the prohibition era. Cathy Mitchell's grandfather, Jonathan Sweetwater ran the business."

"Really?" Lisa scanned all the church-going, barn-dancing folks in the room. "I mean, I didn't picture people in this town even drinking. It's part of the Bible belt, right?"

"We all attend church on Sunday, but any other night of the week it's okay to indulge. Of course, most of the townspeople only drink for medicinal purposes." Eric half bowed, his eyes dancing around the room at various people.

Was it true? Did these people drink? She'd made the trek here to find a family to adopt her child that was devoid of the demons she grew up with. Scanning the crowd, she eyed a few various couples, but did they drink to excess then repent about it on Sunday?

"And if you want to know who partakes and who abstains, just ask Cathy Mitchell. She doesn't like to gossip, but she'll still tell you." He winked down at her.

"So I've heard," Lisa teased, poking him in his side.

"That's right; you're a sophisticated New York City girl. Nothing gets past you." Eric took a swig of punch.

"From what I understand, you were a city boy for a while yourself."

"Yes, that's true." Eric's playful grin disappeared and his eyes cast over with a haunting gaze before he shook his head and placed his cup back down on the table.

A brunette woman approached and patted Eric on the shoulder. "Good to see you here."

Eric scratched his temple. "Yes, well, you know how persuasive my mother can be. Oh, Connie, this is Lisa Mortan." He scooted Lisa into his side as if introducing his girlfriend. Connie's eyes drifted to his hand on Lisa's waist, causing Lisa's face to flame.

"It's a pleasure to meet you," Connie said. "I'm Mr. Gaylord's receptionist."

"It's nice to meet you, too." Lisa tucked a stray piece of hair behind her ear and fought an internal war between leaning further into Eric or pulling away.

The music changed from a hectic, foot-stomping beat to a mellow couple's song. Eric took Lisa's hand once more. "You want to dance?"

Perhaps Judy was right. It was a party and her troubles would be waiting at the door. "Sure."

"See you at the office," Eric called to Connie before he spun Lisa around then brought her close to him, slipping one hand into her right, and the other around to the small of her back.

The room spun with music, his cologne, and the

sway of his hips. And boy, his hips moved with rhythm like no man she'd ever known. The lights dimmed and couples danced on all sides of them. He moved out and back in, spun her around then guided her back to him.

"Wow, you can dance." Lisa eased into his embrace.

"Someone told me in college that a corporate man should know how to dance, so I took some classes. It's come in handy a few times."

"So, you've used this ploy on other girls," she teased.

He dipped her. "Nope, you're the first."

"I should feel special then."

"Absolutely." Lifting her up, he rested his chin on the top of her head and moved side to side.

She wished the music would never end. For the first time in weeks, perhaps months, her heart didn't feel like it was going to drop down to her stomach from the weight of sadness. But feeling good wasn't part of the plan. She was here to find a family for her baby, not fall for some guy she could never have.

Eric moved his head close to her ear. "I'm glad Mom talked me into coming. I was hesitant, but I have to admit this is good."

She couldn't tell if his voice was hoarse from emotion or talking over the music, but she didn't want to shrug from his arms to look.

"Tell me, or was it too painful?" Eric asked.

Lisa followed his sway. "What?"

"What happened to you back in New York?" Eric leaned his head back and caught her gaze.

"It wasn't like that. I'm not some damsel in distress. I wouldn't stick around if I was being abused. It was one night, our last night together that he grabbed my arm. And I walked."

A smile creased his lips. "It's nice to meet a girl that can stand on her own two feet, who'll stick up for herself."

Lisa shrugged, not sure what to say. "I'd never stick around if something like that was going on. I learned a long time ago life is too short and complicated for that kind of mess. I'd prefer to work things out on my own than cling to something unhealthy." The words flowed from her mouth as quickly as he asked the questions. *Too much.* She needed to shut her mouth. She wasn't ready to tell anyone, not until she made up her mind about the baby.

The music ended and she retreated from his embrace. "I, uh, I need to get home. Still have to finish unpacking. Thanks for entertaining the new girl for a bit, but I'm sure there are a ton of women waiting for a dance with you." She glanced around to emphasize her point. "I'll see you tomorrow at the opening."

Lisa nearly tripped over her own feet leaving the dance floor, music, Sweetwater punch, and Eric behind.

"Wait. I'll walk you to your car," Eric said, catching up to her before she'd made it to the door.

"Don't worry about it. Tough girl from New York, remember? You stay with Judy. I can't let anything happen to my new partner. But I'll see you soon." She snatched her coat from the deer horn coat tree and stepped outside. Her troubles were there, waiting for her, and in the cold night air, all the fear and anxiety returned.

She managed to get one arm into her coat before she reached the walkway, and the other before the warm tears dripped down her cold cheeks. This wasn't the plan. She needed to find a family, have the baby then get back to her life in New York with no one ever finding out she was pregnant in the first place.

It's best this way. She rubbed her belly, wishing she could hold the child in her arms, to comfort it from all this, but like Mark said, she didn't have a single motherly instinct. The child needed a family, and she was unfit to be a mother.

CHAPTER NINE

Eric watched Lisa hot-foot it to her car. Her hips swayed and her heels clicked in the night. He wanted to run after her and tell her he was ready to give dating a chance, but he stayed rooted in the doorway. When they danced, her warmth invited him closer. He wanted to pull her curvaceous, firm body into his arms and tell her he didn't want to live in the past anymore, but was he truly ready? Perhaps her leaving was for the best.

His phone buzzed in his pocket. Retrieving it, he noticed five new messages. Scrolling through the numbers, he realized they were all work related. Of course, besides his mother, that was all the calls he received. It was all he'd wanted. Until tonight.

For once he wasn't distracted by his phone, email, or networking opportunities. Instead, he longed to return to the dance floor with Lisa, but without the loud music or people. Only the two of them, swaying against each other while he listened to her sweet voice tell him of her life. He wanted to know everything. Her favorite food, favorite movie, even her favorite flower.

He pulled his car keys from his pocket, but then

shoved them back in. It was too soon. They'd just met, and the way she stiffened in his arms to his inquiry about what happened in New York caused a thrum of warning in his mind. There was more to the story.

"Going somewhere?" His mother's voice traveled from over his shoulder to his cold ear.

"Yes. As requested, I made an appearance. I gave it my all, but it's tough to be here."

"Didn't look so tough from where I was standing." She grasped his arm, tugging him to face her. "From what I saw, two people were quite infatuated with each other. Your facial expressions and body language screamed that fact to everyone in that room. Heck, I felt the fire ignite between you two from across the dance floor. The kind that people search their entire lives to experience, if only for a moment."

"You sound like one of those chick flicks you enjoy making me watch."

"Ha, you love them as much as I do and you know it. You're nothing but a big romantic at heart. Problem is that guilt was a tent over your heart for so long, you don't know how to feel anymore."

Eric ran a hand through his hair, tugging the roots to alleviate some of the tension. "I don't know. My chest is tight. I haven't felt like this in a long time, if ever. It...scares me."

"My son. Captain of the football team, valedictorian, and fighter of rights is afraid to hold a girl's hand." His mother gave him a sappy smile.

"Don't tease me."

"I don't mean to. I only wanted to convey that you

are one of the bravest men around here. Yet, anytime a girl so much as smiles at you, I think you'd run across the ocean to avoid seeing her again. With Lisa, it's different. I see your struggle. You want to stay. Don't let fear keep you from something great." His mother squeezed his upper arms. "I'm telling you, the chemistry between you two is undeniable."

"What makes you so sure we belong together? There were thousands of women in New York City and none of them captured my attention. Why now? Why her?"

His mother chuckled. "First off, you're loyal. You might not have loved Mary Lynn anymore, but you'd never cheat on her. Second, why not her? What don't you like about her?"

Eric paused and thought for a moment. "I don't know her well enough yet to answer that."

"Then tell me what you do like about her."

Eric sighed. "This is ridiculous."

"Humor your old mother."

His mother trembled from the cold, so he removed his jacket and wrapped it around her shoulders. "You shouldn't be out here in the night air without your coat."

"You're avoiding the question," she accused.

"Fine. I like that she left that SOB that got rough with her. That she isn't weak and needy. That she's beautiful, intelligent, caring. Did you know she asked me why the kids weren't at the Hoe Down tonight?"

She shook her head. "She's observant and caring, that's for sure. If you like all these things about her, why are you hesitating?"

Eric shifted between his feet. Struggling with questions of the heart wasn't something comfortable to face. Books, laws, and facts were easy, people and emotions not so much. "There's a connection, as if we have stuff in common, but I don't even know what they are. Heck, I don't really know anything about her other than her name."

His mother's face softened into the loving, empathetic expression he'd known all his life, her smile warm and understanding. "That's what dating is for. Now, listen to your mother. Go for it."

"What about the shop? I haven't seen you so motivated in years. You've been lonely since dad died. If things don't work out...I don't want to mess this up for you."

"We're all adults. There's nothing to worry about. If something happens, we'll deal with it, but don't miss out on love because you want to avoid the possibility that something might go wrong."

Eric huffed. "Love is a strong word. We just met."

"Yes, it is, but you're two grown adults that have obviously both struggled in your past. You're both holding onto grief and secrets you don't want the other to know."

"So, I was right. There's more to the story about what happened in New York, but I don't want to get involved in something messy like that again. I screwed up last time. I don't have the strength to go through all that again. I don't want to have to save someone and take care of them. I'm not good at it."

Judy stroked his shoulder. "No, hon, you're too good at it."

Eric leaned against the banister that bordered the front porch, thinking.

"Listen," Judy continued, "you both need to get to know each other before all the dirty laundry is aired. See if this is all real enough to fight for. Go on a date. Hold hands. Kiss her, before all the mess is shared."

Kiss her? He'd almost leaned in right there in the middle of the dance floor, in front of the entire town, to steal one taste of her luscious, pink lips. *Dating?* It couldn't be that complicated. Of course, the only girl he'd ever really dated was Mary Lynn.

CHAPTER TEN

Lisa hit the *cash* button on the register and the drawer popped open once more. It had only been a little over a week since she'd arrived in Sweetwater and already she'd found a home. A place where warm hugs and smiles greeted her, along with polite conversation and more interest in her personal life than she was used to, but it was magical. A place anyone would be happy raising a child.

Judy ushered a woman with short, white-blonde hair to a credenza. "You'll want to see this, Wanda."

"I recognize those candlesticks," Wanda said. "They're from the Mitchells. Her relative stole them in a divorce from my family. I'll take them both."

Judy's mischievous grin told Lisa she'd planned on that sale from the start. Her partner was shrewd in business, for sure.

Eric squeezed between Lisa and the back wall. "Things are going great. Maybe now the town will stop calling you two *the crazy ladies*." He winked, his playful grin spread across his face. One she'd grown accustomed to him popping by each day at lunch and after work to check on their progress. But today was different, he'd been in a great mood, helping to police people at the door, politely instructing them to stamp the mud from their shoes. He even cleaned up spills from the refreshments they'd served. He was a hard worker and surprisingly domestic. Of course, half the sales came from the cougars in town wanting to paw at him. He took it all in good stride, though.

When the buzz died down, Lisa finally had an opportunity to approach him. "Eric, do you have a second?"

He turned and touched her elbow. "Sure, anything for the girl who got my mother out of the house and back to life."

Had I done that? Picturing Judy anything but lively, fun, and somewhat mischievous didn't seem possible. Her constant nudging to give Eric a chance complicated things, though. Lisa found herself drawn to spending time with Eric, seeking him out each time he'd enter the store to help, but always remaining far enough away that she wouldn't be tempted by his charm. It wasn't working. "Listen, about last week. If I was rude when I left the dance..."

"Don't worry about it." He smiled, but not the kind that lit up the room. "Let's finish up so we can celebrate. Mom said you'd be joining us."

"Yes, I said I would." She straightened the merchandise on the counter, attempting to avoid his gaze.

He brushed passed once more, his cologne engulfing her in a sensory overload. Placing a hand on each of her shoulders, he leaned in and whispered,

"Not like you had a choice, darling," he said, mimicking his mother.

For a second, his touch chased away the loneliness. "No, I guess I didn't."

"Time to close shop," Judy called.

Eric let go and backed away, offering his arm. "Shall we?"

"You two go ahead. I'm going to lock up," Judy offered.

"Are you sure?" Lisa asked, while grabbing her purse from under the front counter.

"Of course." Judy gave her dismissive wave, sending them on their way.

White lights strung from building to building illuminated the front walk and sparkled off the fresh snow covering the trees and grass, but the roads and walkways had already been cleared.

"I hadn't even realized it snowed." Lisa chuckled. "I guess it was a busy day."

"Yes, and a lucrative one. You ladies aren't so crazy after all." Eric tapped the end of her nose with his finger. As he led her down the walkway, she admired the quaint little town, a romantic backdrop reminiscent of a Hollywood movie set. A gust of wind blew between two buildings, sending a chill through her. Eric wrapped his arm around her shoulder and snuggled her against him. "Cold?"

Her body instantly heated. "Just chilled from the wind. I'm fine now."

"Good." He kept her close to his side while they made their way to the other end of the block.

"This place looks like a dream. New York is beautiful at Christmas time, but this town must be beyond amazing during the holidays."

He squeezed her shoulder. "Small towns definitely have charm. And you're right. At Christmas, there is no other place on earth like Sweetwater." He paused for a moment then said, "Did Mom tell you why I left New York?"

"No." She looked up, watching the white lights glint off his eyes.

He smiled. Their feet stopped moving and they stood beneath a tree, its arched branches twinkling overhead. He rubbed her arms from shoulder to elbow. "Yeah, I discovered it wasn't for me. I prefer it here, near Mom and the quiet of the country."

"I like the quiet here, too," she mumbled. Her eyes dropped to his lips before she averted her gaze and stepped back. "What did you do while you were there?"

"I was a partner in a law firm." His voice trailed off for a moment then he shook his head and shot a sideways glance her way. "Do you miss New York? Are you planning on returning?"

"I don't know." Images of her former life flickered through her mind, sending a mist of gloom into her soul. "I guess it depends on how it goes here."

"Then we'll have to make sure things go well. The shop, I mean." He shuffled forward, closing the distance between them, and tucked a stray hair under her hat.

Could she really stay? Memories of her life in New York flooded her mind. Did she want to go back to that? To the long days at a museum, looking at art that didn't inspire her, long nights waiting for Mark to return home after his business meetings. And worst of all, the look of horror in his eyes when she told him she was pregnant.

She turned on her heels but he caught her wrist, causing her to flinch.

"Sorry." He released her arm and stepped around to face her. "You never have to fear me." He placed his knuckle under her chin and nudged her face higher. "The thought of anyone marring such a beautiful face is a crime. One I'd definitely want to prosecute."

Her pulse quickened, his musky aroma teasing her to return his touch, but the thought of his inevitable rejection when he learned of the baby drove her to retreat. "Yes, well. It's over now and I'm tough." The chill in the air stung her ears, so she tugged her cap down. "What about you? Think you'll ever go back?"

Eric slipped his fingers into hers and tugged her toward a side street. "No. New York was just a place to hide. It's a long story, but let's just say I failed someone," he rasped. "Mom's been trying to make me let go of things for a while, but it's been tough. I think that's part of the reason she started the business with you. For weeks she spoke about your emails and phone calls. I knew she was up to something before you even arrived."

"I'm sorry. I had no idea." Lisa lowered her head to hide the flame on her face, and the fact that she was lying. Judy had been more than obvious.

"Don't be. At least Mom has good taste." His hand

squeezed hers twice before they reached the car. "She says I need to take a chance. Live life to the fullest and all that."

Her heart quickened at his words. "Sounds like good advice."

He swung her around and cupped the back of her neck. She leaned back, sandwiched between the car and a strong, intelligent, sweet, caring, and giving man. His lips brushed hers and heat radiated down the back of her neck all the way to her toes. "I've wanted to do this since I first saw you in the shop, but wouldn't admit it to myself," he mumbled against her lips. "Apparently Mother knows best. But don't tell her I said that." His minty breath warmed her mouth. Stroking her cheek with his thumb, he tipped her head back and pressed his lips to hers. A jolt of electricity shot through her arms and legs, lighting a dark place in her soul. Her body awakened, as if it had been sleeping for centuries.

"Wait—" Before she had a chance to protest further, he parted the seam of her lips, dipping his tongue into her mouth. She melted into him. Strong, yet gently, he caressed her back, setting her skin ablaze with need and want. Her hands clung to him and she surrendered. Hugging tight against him, her tongue, and hands, explored him with enthusiasm. They were pressed against the car, with no care of what town gossip watched. In their own little world, anything seemed possible.

Both his hands cradled her face and he moaned before breaking the kiss. "Wow."

Breathless, she just nodded, not knowing what to

say. The world slowed into a wintery blur around them, as if they'd been lost in a tunnel of passion.

"I'm looking forward to a lot more of that." He kissed her forehead and opened the door. Once she caught her breath, her head spun with the knowledge that she had to stop this. She had to confess the truth.

He slid into the car and hit the start button, revving the cold engine to life. "I'm glad you came to Sweetwater. It's been awhile since I've met anyone that caught my interest, and well, you certainly do that."

Tell him the truth before this goes too far. This was wrong. She needed to be honest with him, that she was only in town to find a couple to take her baby. He'd hate her for it, she knew. What mother gave up her child?

Opening her mouth, she turned to him, but he captured her hand and kissed each of her knuckles, melting her resolve to goo. The attention was intoxicating. If things were different, she could fall hard for this man, a man with a family, friends, and loved ones in a small town where everyone knew their neighbors. But things weren't different. She was carrying another man's baby and it wasn't fair to him. He'd certainly leave the minute she told him. What man would ever want a woman pregnant with another man's baby? Geesh, it sounded like a bad episode of Jerry Springer. *Okay, they're all bad*, she mused.

"What are you thinking about?" Eric asked, leaning closer. "If you're worried about this," he gestured between them, "because you work with Mom, don't be. Even if we find that we don't want to pursue anything, it's okay. Besides, Mom practically shoved us together. She won't have a problem with it. You see, she had my head spinning about this amazing, tough, cultured, sexy woman, but she didn't get it right, not completely. We're the same, both wounded and tentative, but I think we should give it a try." He glanced her way and she knew he could read every emotion on her face. He saw the wounds, but probably thought it was because she had been slapped around by some guy.

If she was going to make a clear break, this was her chance, stop it before it went any further. For now, she could use the shop as an excuse. Then, when she was ready she'd share the truth with Judy first, then Eric.

His thumb rotated over her hand, rubbing in small circles. Oh, dear God. His touch alone jumbled her mind. Mark detested any public displays of affections and refused to hold her hand, ever. The sensory overload was clouding her judgment.

Before Lisa had a chance to say a word, the car rolled to a stop in front of Judy's house. He shut off the car and turned sideways. Slipping his hand behind her head, he captured her lips once more. His soft, strong lips, lingering warm tongue, and the inexplicable draw she felt filled her heart with joy. A feeling she hadn't experienced in years, if ever.

His embrace tightened, sealing any space between them, but then he released her and got out of the car. He appeared at her door and opened it for her.

Resting her hand on her fluttering stomach, she realized it wasn't about her anymore. She wasn't her selfish mother. She'd be the kind of woman to sacrifice all for her child. Hadn't she come so far already? Perhaps she would keep the baby and never return to New York. This place would be great for starting a family and she wouldn't ruin it because of hormones and loneliness.

The door opened and she stepped out. With all the will she could muster, she stood on shaking legs, but didn't take his arm. "You're right. I do work with your mother." She couldn't meet his eyes. "So, we should stop this before it goes too far. You're attractive and amazing, but I can't jeopardize my relationship with my partner by dating her son. That's just a bad combination."

His eyes morphed from a twinkling happiness to a dull far-off stare. Rejecting him tore through her heart. The battered pieces begged her to stay with him regardless of the consequences, but this was the right thing to do.

"I see." He stepped back, eyeing her for a moment then ushered her forward. She shuffled up the walkway, but halfway up, he blocked her path. "I don't buy it. I felt the passion in our kiss."

The front door swung open and there was Judy, standing in the center of the light shining through the opening.

"This isn't over," he muttered. "You're going to tell me the truth, or I'll find out what it is on my own. I won't stand back and let something go wrong again."

CHAPTER ELEVEN

The earthy tones, smells of home-baked goods, and the roaring fire in the living room invited them into Judy's home.

"If you'll excuse me for a moment." Lisa followed the hall to the powder room, her heart still aching at the look on Eric's face. What had she done?

The day had taken its toll and now the emotions weighted down her exhaustion even more. Taking a hand towel, she moistened it with cool water under the faucet and pressed it to the back of her neck. She leaned against the counter in an attempt to relieve the dull ache in her low back that had started earlier in the day. *Too much standing. Mental note: wear flats to work from now on.*

Eric's raised voice drew Lisa's attention and she placed the towel on the rack then inched the door open.

"I know you're trying to help. Heck, you had me convinced she was the girl of any man's dreams before she'd even arrived. We all know you're cunning, Mother."

A gasp that could only be Judy's accentuated

denial echoed down the hall.

Eric laughed bitterly. "Oh, please. You can sell anything to anyone. I've seen you work magic to make things happen in this town. You've got a way about you. But I'm your son. I see right through it."

"Was I wrong?" Judy asked.

"About what?" Eric's voice dropped to a hoarse whisper.

"Isn't she the woman of your dreams?" Judy's question lingered for several moments.

Lisa nudged the door open further for a chance to hear his response.

"Yes," Eric mumbled.

Lisa's heart betrayed her and soared to the top of the town clock tower. She crept into the hall, part of her hoping he would say more. The floor squeaked and she jumped, pressing her back against the wall. *That was louder than a pig in heat*, she thought, remembering the expression she'd heard a few times since coming to Sweetwater County.

"Then fight for her," Judy whispered. "We're in here, dear," she called out.

Lisa straightened her coat and sauntered to the living room, her smile light, with no hint she'd overheard a word of their conversation.

Would he fight for her? No one had ever fought to keep her around. They'd always left, without a care for what would happen to her.

Eric snatched his coat off the back of a dining chair. "I forgot I've got an early client tomorrow. You ladies enjoy your celebration." He nodded to Lisa and she returned the gesture before he leaned in to kiss Judy's cheek. "Night, Mom."

"Goodnight, son. Remember what I said." She walked him to the door while Lisa's fingers traced where his lips had been only a few moments ago.

That familiar loneliness nipped at her soul. It wasn't exactly loneliness, but a mixture of guilt and embarrassment. Stroking her belly, she wondered if she had the strength to face everyone. Judy, Eric, the whole town. She'd left New York, so her friends wouldn't see how she'd screwed up. And if they had, Mark would've figured out quick that she didn't have the abortion. Would he really come after her like he'd threatened?

"What'cha thinking about? You gonna stoke the fire with your x-ray vision or something?" Judy asked with her normal sarcastic, yet enchanting twang.

"What?" Roused from her thoughts, the dull ache returned to Lisa's back so she shuffled to the dining chair where Eric's coat had just been and lowered to the seat.

Judy scooted a chair next to her and sat down, taking Lisa's hands in her own. "You know, Eric went through a rough time in New York. He went there looking for something and lost himself for a while. He's a good man, though. Any girl would be lucky to have him."

"Oh, Judy." Lisa could feel tears glistening in her eyes. "Believe me, I have no doubt, but it isn't that simple." Lisa fought the rising lump in her throat, threatening to crack her voice. "Tell me more about Eric. I'd like to know. You only told me about how handsome he was, and gentle and kind. A strong willed person with ambition, I think is how you phrased it, but family always came first. But if so, why did he leave you and go to New York in the first place? What happened to him?"

"Oh, hon, that's not my tale to share. But if you two don't let go of the past, you'll both miss out on something great."

"Like you did?" Lisa squeezed Judy's hands. "Tell me more about James."

"Well, it was a long time ago."

Lisa couldn't help but smile at the familiar twinkle in her partner's eye. It had to be a family trait. "And you remember it as if it were yesterday, right?"

"Perceptive girl, aren't you? Too bad you're not so observant when it comes to yourself."

"Judy..." Lisa started.

Judy leaned back, her hands slipping from Lisa's. "Okay, okay. I get it. You want the old woman to butt out. I guess I am a little pushy. My son knows me too well. Too bad he doesn't realize we're a lot alike. So, you want to know about James Benjamin?"

Lisa nodded, knowing reliving the past was hard for her partner, but she wanted to believe that love was real and attainable, even if it wasn't meant for her.

"He was tall and thin, but strong. A hard worker on his daddy's farm. His mother was beautiful, an artist, but she never left the family home long enough to do anything with her talent. We were close, though, his mother and I. She showed me the beauty in the world through her art. When we went to tell his parents we wanted to marry, I thought they'd go nuts, but they didn't. His father left the room, mumbling about how James was ruining his life, but his mother jumped up and hugged me. She said I looked at her son, like she looked at his daddy, as if he was the only man in the world...and he was." Judy sighed. "Until he was reported captured and presumed dead. We'd heard the same thing many times before from friends and family who'd also lost a loved one. It meant the men had died on the front line and their bodies were never recovered."

Judy's gaze went vacant, her thoughts lost in the past. "A gut wrenching emptiness tore my heart in half and I was never the same again. I'd promised to wait for him and I believed he'd make it home, that we'd grow old on the family farm." She wrung her hands together. "But instead, I was never allowed to set foot on the farm again, I was shunned by his family when I married his cousin."

CHAPTER TWELVE

J udy stood, her chair scraping against the hardwood floor. "Come, it's easier to show you the story than to tell it." She led Lisa up two flights of stairs then pulled down a ladder in the ceiling. "Be careful now, I don't want you falling down these steps." Judy nimbly traversed the steps with her skirt hiked up to her knees.

As Lisa stuck her head through the opening, a light flicked on, revealing boxes and old furniture. "Over here," Judy called. A large trunk rested near a porthole style window. The top creaked open and Lisa leaned over to peer in. The strong scent of cedar replaced the mustiness in the cool air. A white gown rested inside.

"This was my hope chest. I know you girls don't have those anymore, but back in my day getting married was an important event, life altering and permanent. We kept all our wishes and trinkets in these cedar chests." Judy lifted the dress, exposing the short train with sheer material covering a satin bodice. The entire gown was hand-beaded with tiny pearls.

"It's beautiful," Lisa gasped, her eyes stinging with tears. Would she ever wear anything so lovely? She'd actually stopped at a dress shop on her way to tell Mark about the baby. "You must have made a beautiful bride."

"I think I looked okay, but I would've been prettier in this gown than the one I wore. You see, this was the dress for my wedding with James Benjamin, not Eric's dad. I couldn't bring myself to wear it when I married his cousin. Somehow it seemed wrong." Judy fingered the delicate beading lovingly. "My grandmother and I spent weeks making this dress, and several months doing the beading."

"You made this? Wow, you're a talented seamstress." Lisa ran her fingers down the silky material.

"Not me, dear. It was mostly my grandmother. When she passed away around the same time I got married, I stopped sewing completely. I think it made me too sad. Too many memories." Judy gazed out the small window as if she saw a previous life then shook her head and replaced the flowing dress into the cedar trunk, slamming it shut.

"I was lonely," she continued, "in the I-don't-know-if-I-can-live-on sort of way. Eric's dad softened the bone-deep pain of losing James, gave me a part of my life back." Judy wrapped her arms around her middle, her eyes showing a glimpse of the grief from so long ago. "I'm glad you didn't live back in my day. You wouldn't have had a choice but to marry that Mark fellow in your condition."

Lisa stared at her, heat flooding her entire body. "How—when..." She lowered her head and fidgeted with the hem of her shirt. "How did you know?"

"Oh dear, from the minute you walked into the store. A mother can just tell. Plus, you touch your belly all the time when you think no one's watching."

Lisa lifted her gaze to meet Judy's. "Does Eric know?"

"It's not my place to tell and he hasn't mentioned it to me." Judy tapped Lisa's hand.

"But if you knew, why'd you try to get us together? He's your son, and I'm—"

"A girl with a baby on the way. I know." Judy smiled. "I was in your way once, too."

"It's not the same." Lisa perched on the side of an antique desk, "I don't want Mark back. He wasn't the man I thought he was." Images of moments in their relationship shot through her mind like a slideshow on fast forward. Those times she'd attempted to make him happy, to keep him from leaving. It wasn't him she loved, it was the idea of having someone by her side. "Actually, I couldn't go back to him even if I wanted to. You were madly in love with James, but I was only in love with the idea of Mark."

Judy's lips quirked up in a strange smirk. "You misunderstand, honey. I *had* to marry Eric's dad. I was pregnant, and back then, such a thing was scandalous."

Lisa cupped her mouth to stifle her loud gasp. "Is Eric's dad James?"

"No. No." Judy waved her hands. "I've never told anyone the whole story so I'm afraid I'm not doing a very good job. You see, I was best friends with Michael, Eric's dad. We did everything together. It wasn't romantic in any way, but we were good to each other. The night I received word about James, Michael was there. He held me for hours and then, well, the pain was so bad I wanted to forget." Judy sunk into a worn-out wicker chair, her eyes glistening with unshed tears. "It's something I'll always feel guilty about, but never regret because I have Eric."

Lisa struggled to find words to console Judy, but the sight of her partner's sadness rendered her unable to think. The only words that came from her mouth were, "I'm so sorry."

"Oh, don't be. It was a long time ago. My point in telling you this is that you have choices. When I found out I was pregnant with Eric, we didn't have a choice, despite the fact that it was a mistake, two friends mourning a great loss. Michael had a girlfriend he'd planned on marrying and I probably would have remained single the rest of my life because, no matter who came and left in my life, my heart never forgot James."

Lisa had so many questions, but she didn't want to pry, didn't want to make Judy recall her past any more than she had already. Instead, she reached out in an awkward gesture, patting Judy's arm, unsure of how to provide comfort the way the Gaylords did. "I'm so sorry. It must have been tough being married to someone you didn't love."

"Oh, it may not have started out as love, but I grew to love him, as he did I. Heck, we could have divorced later, but we loved each other and the family we'd made. Most never have that, so I consider myself lucky.

I married my best friend, who understood my heart, as I understood his. You see, great men are understanding, caring, and never judgmental. My Eric is just like his daddy. He wasn't always that way, though." Judy chuckled and clapped her hands together. "Oh, he didn't want to turn out like his dad. Nope, he wanted to make something of himself outside this small town, so we sent him to law school and he moved on to New York City, but eventually he realized he wasn't that guy. When Michael got sick, Eric spent more and more time here. I think when his father died, he reflected on all the choices he'd made, and decided New York wasn't the life for him after all. He opened his own law practice here and he's flourished into a happy, successful young man with better priorities."

"Judy, I understand and feel for what you went through, but it was different. You married the father of your baby. You didn't hook up with another man." Lisa ran a finger through the dust on the desk. "I'm pregnant, and I came here to find good parents for my child, but now I don't know what I want to do."

"Oh, I think you do." Judy rose from the chair and knelt in front of Lisa. "I've seen how you hold your belly and hug your middle. You want to feel connected to that little one growing inside you. It doesn't matter how, or by who that it got there, you love that baby just the same. And I can tell you that it doesn't matter if you and Eric work out, or if you and the baby's father get back together, you'll never be lonely again when you have that little one in your arms." Judy tipped Lisa's chin up. "Listen, you can make your own choice and I'll promise you this, I'll be with you the whole way. I always thought if I could help someone through the fear and loneliness of being pregnant and alone, I would. Yes, I had Michael, but we were both grieving for our loss and our mistake. It wasn't until I held Eric for the first time that I really began to heal. Once that happened, nothing else mattered."

"I can't go back to the baby's father. Ever." Lisa sniffed.

"Why? Did he hurt you? Was he rough?" Judy asked.

Lisa squeezed Judy's hands as if to keep herself from fleeing in desperation. "No—yes...well, he became angrier than I'd ever seen him before, but it was worse." Lisa's arms shook and she fought for control. She was stronger than this.

"What?" Judy nudged.

"Mark said that I...that I had to have an abortion and if I didn't, he'd take care of it himself." Lisa took a stuttered breath, fighting against the tears. "He said he'd kill my baby."

Judy stood up and pulled Lisa into her arms. "Oh, child. Shh...he's not going to do any such thing." She rocked Lisa until her sobs calmed then she scooted back and grasped Lisa's shoulder. "Did you go to the police?"

"No. I was shocked and then he just stormed out." The image she'd built of her happy future had crumbled around her in an instant. "I didn't think about calling the police but I know that if I had called them, it would've just made things worse. I'd helped a friend of mine out of a domestic abuse situation, so I know how the system works. No, I did something worse." Lisa bowed her head in shame.

"What could you have done? You were the victim." Judy tensed her grip on Lisa's upper arms. "It's okay, you can tell me."

"I waited a couple of days," Lisa heaved then settled, "then told him I aborted the baby. He believed me. I told him it was too painful to remain in New York City knowing I'd just terminated my pregnancy. He agreed then immediately had me fired." She choked and fought for composure, concentrating on her breathing, the smell of Judy's floral perfume, the sound of the furnace cutting on downstairs, anything to ground herself to this place. After a few moments, she took a deep cleansing breath and continued. "So, you see, I can't return."

Judy rose. "Wait here a second." She disappeared behind an armoire, and Lisa could hear a drawer being tugged open then Judy returned with a white embroidered cloth. "Here, it was one of the handkerchiefs my grandmother made me embroider by hand. She always thought a lady should be an artist in all things domestic. I'm afraid I failed miserably."

Lisa chuckled. The pink and blue circles resembled flowers but she wasn't sure. "But it's so beautiful."

"Don't lie to me. We've come too far today." Judy winked and walked to the ladder. "I think it's time for some hot cocoa." She grabbed the side railing then paused. "Just one question."

Lisa dabbed at her eyes with the handkerchief.

"What is it?"

"When are you going to tell Eric the truth? It's a tight group here. I'm afraid in another month or so you won't be able to hide under those baggy shirts and sweaters anymore, and it would be best if Eric heard it from you and not Cathy Mitchell."

CHAPTER THIRTEEN

Eric dumped his briefcase on the kitchen table then went into his living room and sunk into his favorite leather chair. The room was quiet and cool, but he didn't see any reason to build a fire, not when there was no one to share it with.

Restless, he eyed his briefcase. He usually spent his nights working until he stumbled to bed exhausted, but tonight his mind raced of other things, and work didn't interest him. Shoving from the chair, he slid his laptop from his briefcase, grabbed a beer and the television remote, then took his seat again.

He pressed the power button on the remote and the nightly news clicked on. He paid little attention to reports of an accident shutting down the interstate and a shooting in Chattanooga, only wanting the TV on for the white noise. Anything to drown out the silence invading his home and the meandering thoughts of Lisa Mortan.

Facts, that was what he needed. Lawyers researched cases, obtaining details and events that provided the necessary information to make an educated decision. That was what made sense. Not all this talk about trust and love. "Mother and her romantic notions," he mumbled. If Lisa Mortan was hiding something, he'd find it.

Fingering the laptop keyboard for the tiny bumps on *F* and *J*, he entered in his passcode. Taking a swig of his beer, he eyed the television to see if there were any criminal trial updates or sports stats, but the newscasters were still droning on about some foreign policy disagreement they'd been harping about for months.

The wireless finally connected and he typed *Lisa Mortan* into the search engine of his browser. The tiny illuminated circle spun for a second then a bunch of *Lisa Mortans* popped up. A school teacher, stripper, body builder, and even a nun. It seemed everybody had an online presence nowadays.

He cleared the search and typed in, *Lisa Mortan New York City Museum*. He clicked the top line and found some philanthropic article about a man named Mark. The article included a photo of the man, with Lisa standing beside him. They didn't look happy, more like statues posed for a promotional piece.

He took another swig of his beer, coating his constricting throat with cool hoppy and ale flavors. A man's equivalent to a woman's bubble bath, beer was soothing, relaxing, and relieved tension. Of course, he only ever drank one. He'd seen too many marriages destroyed by alcohol and drugs, some of them his own clients. Besides, after that car wreck his junior year, he'd decided to never drink to excess again. Lesson learned, the hard way.

Scrolling down through the web page, he read more about Mark Brenson and his accomplishments, with a short bio about his fiancé, Lisa Mortan. He was her fiancé? Eric thought. He had to have been the one who put that bruise on Lisa's wrist. He cracked his knuckles and read on, learning critical intel about Lisa, like her place of birth.

Typing *Salt Lake City, Lisa Mortan* into the search bar, he found the names of her father and mother, which led him to an obituary for her father. Eric dug through the internet for hours, uncovering tidbits and putting the pieces together. Newspaper articles, high school yearbooks, newsletters, and blogs yielded a wealth of information.

His heart tightened at the photo of a little girl with no shoes or socks, her hair matted, standing on a street corner waiting for food from a shelter. No name was listed, but it was her. The same hair and large eyes breached the black and white world of the newspaper article, reaching for his soul. A Vietnam vet who suffered from PTSD after the war, much like Mary Lynn's dad had. Had Lisa's father abused her the same way? Had he been a drunk? Had he whipped her with his belt and told her she was nothing?

He couldn't go through that again.

He shoved the computer from his lap onto the side table and bent over, resting his elbows on his knees. His head throbbed with tension. "How?" he whispered into the night. How did she go from being nearly homeless to an educated woman living in New York

City? How had she paid for college?

College?

He yanked the computer back onto his lap and searched for colleges and universities in Salt Lake City. Entering each one in the search bar with her name, he came up empty-handed.

Wait, a girl with no money wouldn't be able to afford a university.

He typed *Salt Lake City Community College Lisa Mortan* into the search bar and found a link to more of her online footprint over the years. According to the search results, she'd worked full time as well as completed a scholarship project, all while attending school. He also assumed she cared for her father during that time, based on the date of his death and her place of residence. She fought and clawed her way to a senior college, graduating salutatorian.

It wasn't until her father's death, though, that she moved to New York City. Based on the dates, she must've started dating Mark almost immediately following her father's death. Had she been lonely, just wanting to find someone? He could understand that. If everything he'd just learned was true, she was the only woman he'd ever met with so much inner strength.

His cell rang with the theme song to *Leave it to Beaver*. Retrieving it from his briefcase, he answered, "Hey, Mom."

"Hey to you. How you doing?" his mother replied in her sweet, sympathetic tone.

What a loaded question. "I'm fine," he lied. The turmoil in his stomach mixed with the beer and lack of food, conjuring something dreadful.

"You should've stayed for dinner, instead of having a temper tantrum," she scolded playfully. "Glad you've calmed down. I've never seen you so worked up."

How could he tell her that she'd bulldozed through his ten foot thick emotional dam he'd put up, keeping out pretty, sweet women for the last couple of years, and now all his emotions were flooding out at once?

"It's okay to move on, son. She's gone. You deserve to be happy now."

"It's not that..." He sighed. "Yes, the guilt's still there, but it's more than that."

"What is it?"

He gulped around the boulder of fear lodged in his throat. "What if I fail her, too?"

"Oh, son," she sighed. "You didn't fail Mary Lynn. And even if you had, you can't spend the rest of your life avoiding love because you don't want to fail someone else."

"What about you? I did some digging. Those letters Lisa and I found are from a man prior to when you and Dad married. He lived here in this town, didn't he?"

Silence.

"What? You're allowed to dig into my love life, but I can't ask about yours?" Eric lifted his voice to ensure she caught his teasing tone.

"I...it's a long story."

Eric chuckled. "I doubt I'm going to sleep anytime soon."

A long breath sounded into the receiver. "He was a man I loved dearly before I married your dad."

Eric braced himself. He'd thought long and hard about whether he wanted to know the answer to his next question. "Based on the dates I saw on those letters, it was only weeks before you married Dad. How did things turn around so fast?"

After a moment, she replied, "He died. In the war."

The pain in her voice tugged at his heart. He wished he'd waited to ask until he was by her side. She was an amazing mother, who always gave good advice, even when he didn't want it, who'd comforted him through the years. Now, it was his turn. "I'm so sorry, Mom. Something tells me he was special. Why didn't you ever mention him before?"

"Your dad and I never spoke about him. Not in all the years we were married. Oh, he was always there, but it pained us both too much to speak of him aloud."

Eric rubbed the back of his neck and leaned against the wall, eyeing his monochromatic brown living room. "Dad knew him, too?"

"Yes, they were cousins and best friends," her voice cracked with emotion, but the lawyer in him had to push.

"Mom, the dates...I'm not dumb. You and dad had to marry, didn't you? I was born seven months or so after your wedding."

"You knew?" she gasped.

"Of course, since I was, like, twelve."

"You never said anything," she replied.

"No. If you wanted me to know, you would've talked about it." He slumped back in his chair, willing himself to ask the question that really mattered. "Mom, is he my biological father? If so, what happened?"

"No." She chuckled awkwardly. "Wow, that's the popular conclusion today. Michael was your biological and devoted father. He loved you. Heck, you two are so much alike, it's not even funny. No, the man who wrote those letters died in the war and I married your father shortly after."

"You had to marry him because of me, right? Did you ever regret it?" He held his head in his free hand.

"Never."

CHAPTER FOURTEEN

Bright morning sun broke through the grey clouds that had hovered over Lisa's life for the last week, the golden rays highlighting the sign for Gaylord, Attorney at Law.

Her stomach rumbled, reminding her the baby needed food, but she couldn't bring herself to eat. Not with the eminent confrontation awaiting her.

Glancing at the side street leading toward the center of town, she sighed, her heartwarming at the sight of *Cathy Mitchell* driving past. She could put names to so many faces already. After five years in New York City, she didn't even know her neighbor's name.

Taking a deep breath, she shoved her car door open. With determined steps, she marched to the front door. *What if he hates me and it ruins my relationship with Judy?* Of course, it would be far worse if he learned about the baby on his own. Awkward moments and judgmental eyes were better than weeks of deception and lies.

"Excuse me," a girl spoke from behind.

"Oh, sorry." Lisa swung the door to the building open, allowing the girl to enter ahead of her then she, too, stepped into the world of 'Gaylord the attorney.' A side of Eric she couldn't picture. Most of the attorneys she knew were evil bloodsuckers that wanted nothing more than money and prestige, at least the ones that were friends with Mark and danced in the same upper class social circles.

A vacant desk stood between Eric's office and the waiting room. A light perfume fragrance lingered and Lisa was reminded of the woman she'd met the night of the hoe down.

"Are you here to see Mr. Gaylord, ma'am?" the young girl asked her, taking a seat in one of the chairs lining the wall.

"Um...no. I mean, yes. But I don't have an appointment."

The distinctive sound of a chair scooting across wood floors echoed into the waiting room from Eric's office. *Too bad, looks like he's busy*, she thought with a sigh of relief. Now, she could just leave a message and have him stop by later. Their discussion could wait until lunch.

Before she could slip back out the front door, Eric ambled into the room with a welcoming smile, his navy suit jacket accentuated his broad shoulders and narrow waist, and she thought he looked good in the blue jeans and flannel he wore while working around the store.

His blue eyes danced between her and the young girl. His smile tightened into a firm line. "Please have a seat in my office," he said to the girl, lifting his arm to direct her into the room behind him. "I'll be there momentarily."

The girl pulled her sleeves over her knuckles. "I...I can come back later."

"No need. You have an appointment and I'll just be a moment." His warm smile spread across his face again and she bowed her head before shuffling into his office.

What could she need an attorney for? Lisa thought. The girl couldn't be more than sixteen.

"What're you doing here?" He closed the distance in two long strides.

"I wanted to talk to you, but I can see you're busy." She backed away and headed for the door. "I'm sorry. I should've called."

His hand covered hers as she grabbed the knob. "Wait." Warm breath caressed the back of her neck and her body erupted in goose bumps. He hooked one of his fingers into hers and tugged her hand free of the handle then turned her around to face him. "You're right; I can't talk now, but how about lunch? I have a break at one."

She managed a nod.

He leaned over and kissed her cheek. "Until one then."

Every neuron fired at once and her brain turned to mush. She cleared her throat. "One," she said before she bolted from the office and into her car. Still breathless, she pulled into a parking place in front of the store and rushed inside, managing to maneuver to the back kitchen without knocking anything over.

"I hope you're ready, dear," Judy said. "A bus of tourists is in town. I handed out flyers and the coordinator said they'd be here in," she glanced at her watch, "ten minutes." Judy grabbed her mug from the counter, pausing before taking a drink as she looked at Lisa. "You look a little pale. You feeling okay?"

"Yeah. I just...I tried to talk to Eric, but he was busy. He said he'd stop by at one for lunch." Lisa set her purse and keys in the pantry then shut the door. "Judy, I'm so sorry about all this. I hope this doesn't cause any issues between the two of you."

"Don't worry. It'll be fine. You don't need to be stressing now, either." Judy gave her a stern, motherly look. "Have you called Dr. Hendricks yet? You need to start caring for yourself and that little one."

"No, not yet. I'll call him today." Sweat slicked her palms with the thought of facing a doctor when she showed up without a husband. *It doesn't matter*, she reminded herself. Life wasn't about her anymore. It was about the baby.

The front bell jingled and a herd of people poured into the little store.

Judy's eyebrows arched and she wagged her finger. "Don't you forget, now," she chided before heading toward the front of the shop.

Lisa smiled and held up her hands in surrender. "I won't."

The tourists devoured the antiques, buying nearly every trinket, linen, and knick-knack, anything they could carry onto the bus, not to mention the furniture they were having shipped to their country cabins or beach houses.

"Wow, what a gold mine," one woman said. "I've wanted to decorate our summer cottage with some rustic accents." She slipped her platinum card from her expensive handbag. Lisa didn't recognize the name stitched into the leather, but it had to be an up-and-coming designer. This woman was the type that wouldn't have anything less.

"Hey, you." A warm hand slipped to the small of Lisa's back and she glanced up to see Eric's bright smile. "Mom said y'all were slammed so I brought you a decaf coffee, one raw sugar."

The fact he took time off to deliver it, let alone knew that was how she liked it, boggled her mind. "Thanks."

Lisa finished the transaction and handed the woman her receipt but the woman's eyes were glued on Eric. "Thank you very much," she said, trying to draw the woman's attention. "And please do come visit us again."

The woman took the receipt and slowly turned to leave, her eyes never leaving Eric. "Oh honey, you can count on it."

Lisa chuckled softly as she watched the woman fumble her way to the exit.

"Listen," Eric said as the next customer in line stepped up to the register, "I was hoping you could steal away for an early lunch. I'm afraid I have to fly out this afternoon. A big client from overseas only trusts me to handle his affairs. Says his ex-wife has too many connections. I have to head to the islands to file some paperwork and then jet to Paris for a few days." He eyed the line of customers weaving through the store. "But doesn't look like you can get away right now, so our talk will have to wait. Sorry."

"That's okay, I understand." Part of her was relieved, but the other part wanted to be done with it. The anticipation from wondering how he would take the news was eating at her and she was afraid if she waited any longer, the harder it would be to face his rejection.

"Can I call you tonight?" he asked.

"Sure, though I don't really want to talk about it over the phone."

The woman at the counter began tapping her French manicured nails next to the register.

"I'll let you go," Eric said, with an apologetic smile, "but I agree. We'll talk when I get back. I need to tell you something, too." He pressed his lips to her forehead, sending heat through her body. How could a simple touch cause so much reaction? Pregnancy. It had to be her crazy hormones again. A man had never set her body on fire before. She'd read about such things in books or seen it in the movies but it had always made her laugh.

"Until later." He backed away to say goodbye to Judy. "Yes, Mom. You do know best." His loud mumble carried through the crowd before he disappeared out the door.

Does he really think I'm his match?

"Any day now," the woman on the other side of the counter huffed.

"Sorry, ma'am." Lisa rang up her items, ran her credit card, and printed her receipt.

The woman snatched the receipt out of Lisa's hand. "I just love these small town people," she muttered. "They're so...southern."

Lisa forced a smile. "Thank you so much, ma'am," she said with a drawl.

CHAPTER FIFTEEN

Eric tossed his suitcase on the third lumpy hotel mattress of the week and fetched the laptop from his briefcase. Then he tugged the heavy curtains open with a swish and eyed the amazing view through the glass door that opened to a small balcony.

The Eifel Tower, lit up like a Christmas tree. A view that would be etched in his mind forever. A view meant to be shared. A view meant for lovers.

What time is it in Tennessee? he wondered. He'd been on airplanes, bouncing between the Bahamas and Paris, tailing a needy client for days. No, it was into weeks now. Why was he putting himself through all this? He knew why. This one case would pay his bills for a year and provide enough left over for pro bono cases, like Ms. Burton. His mind was still battling with his heart over that one. Taking on a case against the largest business owner in Tennessee seemed like a bad idea.

Of course, his mother didn't see it that way. She accused him of avoiding Lisa, knowing how scared he was to share his past with her.

He turned the handle, opening the old door to a

cacophony of honking horns and lively nightlife. Had Lisa ever been to Paris?

Perhaps it wasn't too late. He sat at the desk and opened his laptop. With a few clicks, he was logged on and listening to the ring tone of Skype. He held his breath, wiping his moist palms on his thighs. What was it about this woman? She turned him inside out. He'd been trapped on that long flight with nothing to do but think about her while everyone else slept.

The ring stopped and the video clicked on, showing Lisa's beautiful, happy face. That was why. The Eifel tower at night didn't compare to her intoxicating smile.

"Hi, you," Lisa said.

"Hi, you back," he chuckled.

Lisa quirked her head to the side, her chestnut hair falling over her cheek. "Isn't it the middle of the night there?

"Yeah, I think so." He rubbed his eyes. "I just got in and thought I'd check in on everything back home. The shop going well?"

"Yep. Everything's great. You're missed, though." She smiled. "I mean, your mom wants you to hurry home."

"Just my mother? Not you?"

How needy did that sound? he chided himself silently.

"Especially me," she replied softly.

He relaxed. Those two words providing so much hope that, when he returned, she wanted to see more of him. "Wait, I have to show you something." He stood up, carrying his laptop to the open doorway. "Isn't it beautiful?"

"Wow! That's the view outside your room?" Lisa's voice rose an octave.

"Yep. Have you ever been to Paris?" He turned the laptop screen back around and plopped down on the bed, resting his feet on top of the suitcase.

"No, but I've always dreamed of going. I'd actually planned a trip there for last summer, but, well...things changed." She looked away, as if someone had entered the room, but then she resettled and met his gaze again.

He wanted to see her smile again. "Hey, why don't you take it this summer? I'll probably have to come back to see this client again. I'll bring you with me. That is, if my mom can spare you." He winked.

"I...I don't know if I can." She stumbled over her words.

Too fast. Great. "Well, there's plenty of time between now and then. Maybe we'll be able to work something out."

She forced a smile.

Okay, time to change the subject. "So, what's the big news in town? I'm sure Cathy Mitchell has kept you apprised of all the happenings."

"Of course, she has. I think there's more to her than just gossip, though. Sometimes people act a certain way because they're in pain. They don't want to share what's going on in their own lives, so they turn the focus toward others. Sort of a defense mechanism, I guess."

"Lisa Mortan, you are one wise woman." He

watched her mouth curl into a shy smile, her pearly white teeth shining in the dim light. Yet, there was a sorrow still clouding her eyes. It faded each time they chatted, but slipped back in during the silent moments. The thought of some guy hurting this amazing, smart, giving woman made his blood boil.

"What is it?" she asked.

He blinked. "Oh, nothing. Sorry, just thinking, that's all." There was a knock at his hotel door. "Hey, hang on a sec. I'll be right back." He pushed from the bed, realizing he hadn't even removed his shoes when he came in. Heck, he hadn't done anything but run to the computer to call Lisa. He didn't remember ever being that needy before. Geesh, he needed to tone it down a little or he'd scare her away.

Opening the door, Adam Parez burst in. "Finally, I've been pacing the floor. My wife's now threatening to take my corporation away."

Eric held up his hand. "Hold on a second, please." He took a long breath and went back to the bed. "Hey, you."

"Hey, you back," Lisa chuckled. "I heard. You've got to run."

"Yeah, sorry. Can I call you tomorrow?"

"Sure, but make sure you get some rest. I don't want you returning here exhausted and sick."

"Didn't know you cared," he whispered, setting the laptop on the desk.

Adam cleared his throat.

"Guess you'll have to call me tomorrow night to find out how much," Lisa teased then blew a kiss before the screen went blank.

He closed the laptop and directed his attention to Adam. "Mr. Parez, you do realize it's the middle of the night. If you weren't an old friend, I'd have thrown you out."

"If I wasn't an old friend, I wouldn't warn you."

"Warn me of what?" Eric turned on the lights and sat at his desk chair.

"That you've got it bad." He motioned to the laptop. "Who's got you all twisted up like a lunatic? I've never seen you so...mushy before."

"Oh, please. I don't do mushy. I'm a lawyer," Eric protested.

"You might be a lawyer, and a darn good one, too," Adam said, "but you have a big heart. I'm not sure how you've survived this long in this business."

"If you doubt my lawyer abilities, what are you doing here?"

Adam rolled his eyes. "I don't doubt your abilities, man. You're the only shark I'll trust. I'm just saying, whoever that girl is, sign a pre-nup because you're too in love to see straight."

CHAPTER SIXTEEN

The all too familiar ring of Skype sounded from Lisa's computer. Leaning over the desk, she minimized the spreadsheet Judy had created, highlighting their already impressive profit margin, and clicked the video icon.

Eric's handsome face appeared, his blue shirt accentuating his bright eyes, which gleamed next to the dark background of his hotel room. "Hi, there," he said, his baritone voice drawing her complete attention.

She fluffed her hair and wished she'd dabbed on some lipstick before answering. "Hi, you. How was your day?"

"Terrible, full of arguing and impossible people, and none of them were as beautiful as you are." He winked.

Even through the internet, he caused her knees to feel weak. She scooped her laptop into her arms and shuffled to the bed. "You're still in Paris, right?"

"Yes. I'm sorry. I thought I'd be back by now, but this case is taking longer than I'd thought."

"For the client that came to your room last night?"

Eric nodded. "Yeah. His divorce and child custody case is being settled in the US, but he wanted me to come hold his hand through the negotiation process. He's not very tech savvy, so video conference calls freak him out. If it wasn't for the fact the income he generates keeps my Sweetwater practice afloat right now, I'd refuse."

"Well, I have a feeling you're there for more than the money. He's an old friend, isn't he?"

"How did you know that?" Eric asked.

"Women's intuition." Lisa flicked her wrist as if she possessed magical powers.

"Oh, really?" he teased. "Well, what does your intuition say about me getting home soon?" He rolled his sleeves up to his elbows, as though prepping for heavy lifting, and his strong forearms drew her attention for a moment. The man was muscular for a lawyer.

"I don't know, but I hope you're taking lots of pictures for me," she nudged, her desire to see Paris nearly oozing from her pores. It was a place where dreams came true in her fantasy world.

His lips quirked up on the right side, the way it did when he was about to tease her about something. "No, I don't think I'll take pictures for you."

She gasped with exaggeration. "Why?"

"You want to see Paris, you'll have to agree to come back with me. We don't even have to wait until summer. I'm sure I'll have to return again in the near future. The antique shop should be settled in another four to six months. I'm sure Mom will let you out on good behavior."

Four to six months? By that point, I'll be about ready to pop.

"So, you better get to work if you want to take that trip with me. Did you finish unpacking everything at your house yet?" He narrowed his eyes, looking past her and shifting his gaze high and low. "I don't see any boxes."

She chuckled. "Well, I'm sitting on my bed, complete with a comforter and sheets now. So, no more sleeping on the couch." She fixed her pillows behind her and propped the laptop on her thighs. Just then a swoosh fluttered in her belly and she thought her entire stomach rolled inside out.

"What's wrong? You feeling okay?"

She slipped her hand from her abdomen and nodded. "Yes." *Except, I think the baby I'm carrying by another man just moved for the first time and I want to share it with someone, but I can't share it with you because you don't even know I'm pregnant!*

"You sure? Mom's not working you too hard, is she? She can be a real workhorse. Trust me, I know." His brows furrowed.

"No, it's not that at all."

He scrubbed his chin. "Then what is it?"

She sucked in a long breath and steadied herself. It was wrong to tell him over Skype. It was an in-person kind of conversation for sure, but she couldn't hold it in any longer. The last two weeks, talking every day, seeing him on Skype every night, learning about his family and friends, work and interests…"Eric…I need to tell you something." Her hands and legs began to tremble.

"No way. Remember our deal? Nothing serious until I get home." He sighed. "Listen, it can't be that bad. We both know we have some deep dark secret we need to share, but I'm glad we've had this time to learn more about each other. Mom told me we had a lot in common, but I didn't realize it until we started talking about literature, travel, our favorite movies. That's the kind of stuff that should start a relationship. I didn't want to lead with baggage from the past. This way, we'll know if the challenge ahead is worth the effort."

Could Judy be right? Is Eric the type of man that would stick around even after learning the truth? "You make a valid argument, Attorney Gaylord. I guess I know who I'll hire in the future," she teased.

"Let's hope you never need my services. Being a family attorney, all I see are divorce and child custody cases. Neither of which I want anything to do with in my own life."

His words seared her heart until it felt cold and dark, all hope burned away. "I, uh, better get some sleep. I'm opening the shop in the morning." She fought the rising lump in her throat and tears forming in her eyes. Why did she keep hoping? When would she learn? How insane was she to believe a man would want her after he discovered she was pregnant. It didn't matter, though. She'd already promised herself she'd be the kind of mother who put her child first, above everyone and everything.

"Lisa?"

"Yes?" she choked out, fighting back the tears threatening to spill down her cheeks.

"Whatever it is, you can trust me. It won't send me running, I promise."

She didn't want to do this. She was stronger than this. Yet, all she could do was nod.

He leaned toward the screen, "I wish I was there to hold you right now. I'd hold you all night if you wanted me to."

Her lungs constricted, and she fought to find her breath. She wanted to tell him how much she'd love to fall asleep in his arms. How he was the most loving, giving, amazing man she'd ever known. A man with a family, a job, a kind heart, and a sexy smile. But she couldn't because when he returned and discovered the truth, he'd be gone.

He leaned back and crossed his arms. "I hope you'll think about it, because I'll be home on Friday."

"What?" Lisa bolted up, nearly toppling the laptop from her legs. "I thought you were there until the end of next week."

"I was supposed to be, but I think you need a hug. If I could, I'd be there tonight." His gaze held hers through the screen. "Listen, Mom says you're scared to tell me the truth. Well, you know what? I'm scared to tell you the truth, too. But if we're going to continue forward, we need to get everything out on the table. And Lisa, I want to continue forward. Whatever happened back in New York, leave it behind. Don't let it poison you here. You're safe with me."

He still thinks I'm some abuse victim that had to

run away.

"If you don't believe me, then just ask Mom. She knows best after all." He winked. "At least she always thinks she does." He chuckled then pressed two fingers to his lips and held them out to her. "I'll see you soon."

"Goodnight," Lisa replied and slid her mouse over the button to terminate the conversation. The fantasy world of Paris and Eric Gaylord disappeared and she was left alone in her rented house.

Sliding the laptop to the floor, she rolled over and held her belly, curling into a ball. "It's okay, I'm not alone. I have you."

CHAPTER SEVENTEEN

Eric Gaylord swirled cream into his coffee, dulling the bitter roast. A secretary with long legs and a thick French accent poured another cup of steaming brew and handed it to Adam.

Adam cleared his throat. "You got some place better to be?"

"What?" Eric slipped the cuff of his suit sleeve back over his watch and shook his head. "Um, no."

Adam nodded to his secretary, dismissing her, then hiked his pant legs up and sat in one of the office's leather armchairs. "Seriously?" He gave Eric a skeptical look. "Let's be honest here, Eric. You and I have been through a lot together, and you probably know every dirty little secret I have. So..." He took a sip of his coffee, steam fogging his designer glasses. Slipping them off, Adam pulled a handkerchief from his pocket and cleaned the lenses."...I've got a confession to make."

Eric set his mug down on the coffee table between them and leaned back in his chair, studying his old friend and client. "What's that?"

"I don't need you to babysit me anymore. I know how to run the intercom-thingy, and even if I didn't, I have secretaries that do."

Eric laced his fingers together. "Then why keep me here in Paris for so long?" His temper was beginning to rear its ugly head, probably more from lack of sleep and jet lag than from the situation.

"Do you hear yourself?" Adam tried to look appalled but failed. "I forced you to stay in Paris? I've invited you out every night to see the sights, and...mingle." He winked. "But all you do is race back to your room to chat with that chick on your computer." He took another sip. "If you ask me, you've got it bad, man. Here I thought I'd persuade you to come work for me. Be my own personal attorney. We'd party every night and jet around the world, free and single."

Eric thought about the fast life he'd had in New York. Okay, it was more business dinners and social events than nightclubs and parties. Still, it was exhausting and unfulfilling. "Not interested," he replied.

"Wait. Now, hear me out." Adam held up a hand. "Killer bonuses, great hours, awesome pay, and... fringe benefits. Did I mention the awesome pay?"

"Adam, maybe a few years ago I would've jumped at the chance, but now...I don't know. I guess I'm happy being closer to home at this stage of my life."

"You mean closer to that woman," Adam scoffed. "Fine, I get it. Besides, I think you've lost your edge. That big wig New York attorney that would stop at nothing to reach his goal has disappeared." He took a swig of his coffee.

"You're right. I'm not that person anymore. I work within the parameters of the law, not that I ever broke them before."

"No, but you bent plenty. And boy, could you bluff." A hint of admiration shone in his friend's eyes.

He cringed at the memory of his ruthless nature. "I'll never be that person again. Nothing could make me bend the rules so far again."

"Don't lie to yourself," Adam said casually. "Everyone has a price."

Eric opened his mouth to protest, but Adam quickly lifted his hand to stop him. "Don't even bother arguing. We both know it's true, even if you refuse to admit it." He rubbed his hand through his hair and Eric noticed he still wore his wedding ring even though his divorce proceedings were in full swing.

"You don't really want that life either, do you?" Eric asked. Eric studied his friend for a moment. "I don't get it. Why aren't you back home, trying to work things out instead of here?"

Adam chuckled and shook his head sadly. "I came here hoping to woo her. To give her the attention I didn't for the past ten years. I thought if I brought her here, to this city, she'd, I don't know, feel something again."

"Oh." The regret and loneliness Eric could see in Adam's eyes made him see his friend in a different light than he had the last couple of weeks. Adam wasn't the confident, suave, womanizing businessman he'd thought, but a broken divorcee. Something inside Eric stirred, his desire to go home stronger than he'd ever felt.

"If you've got something special with this girl," Adam said, "then don't screw it up. Don't do what I did. I spent more time on acquisitions and sales than I did with my wife, and now she's hooked up with some writer want-a-be. He's *passionate* and *giving*." Adam made quotation marks in the air with his fingers, something Eric never thought he'd see in his life. "Even my money wasn't enough to keep her with me."

"I'm sorry, man." Eric thought for a moment, trying to find the right words. "Perhaps she's going through something, too. I've seen more than one marriage where the wife looked for something she wasn't getting at home, only to discover it was no better."

"Really?" Adam's face lit up. "Yeah, I mean, not like some writer is going to keep her happy. She doesn't even like to read."

Eric smiled at his friend's newfound hope. "Can I give you some advice?"

"Sure." Adam leaned forward eagerly, resting his elbows on his knees.

"Go home. It's going to be tough to see her with this other guy, but if you want to fight for her, you can't do it from here. Love isn't about the location. It's about your actions."

"I guess all those years in school actually taught you something." Adam reached across the coffee table and slugged Eric's arm. "Now, it's my turn. Can I ask you a question, without you running from the room?"

"Sure." Eric took a tentative sip of his coffee, trying not to gag on the secretary's idea of a medium roast.

"You ready?" Adam ran a finger around the rim of his mug. "I've never pried, but I know how destroyed you were after Mary Lynn's death. You know, it wasn't your fault, man. She had issues. You tried to help, but marrying the girl wouldn't have saved her. You need to let go of the guilt."

Eric's lungs clenched tight. Even her name caused him gut-wrenching pain. "It's not so much the guilt."

Adam's brows furrowed. "Then what is it? Why have you avoided women like the plague ever since the accident?"

"You sure I won't lose my man card for this one?" Eric joked, trying to ease the tension and threat of crumbling in front of his old friend and business partner.

"You're safe." Adam smiled.

"I'm scared. If it hurt that bad to lose someone I cared about, and a little one I didn't even know about, what if I have a wife and child and lose them? I still have night terrors, images of her in the car, the blood, the doctor telling me the baby was dead." Eric's voice broke. "Sorry, man. Never spoke about this aloud, to anyone. You best not judge."

"Eric." Adam gave him a sympathetic look. "It makes perfect sense. Perhaps a year ago I wouldn't have understood what you're saying, but today I do. I know it's not the same, but losing my heart has turned me inside out. It's all I can do to get out of bed and get dressed in the morning. Life hurts sometimes, in an I-want-to-punch-everyone's-lights-out sort of way, but that doesn't mean we stop trying. If you love this woman—"

"I just met her."

Adam laughed. "I knew I loved my wife by our second date, when she told me point blank to get over myself. She was the perfect balance of spunk and beauty. You've talked to this woman for weeks, every night you could. Trust me, man. You love her. So, get your sorry ass on a plane and go tell her how you feel."

Eric took in a jagged breath. "Okay, on one condition."

"What's that?" Adam asked.

"You get your sorry ass on a plane and go tell your wife how you *really* feel." Eric stood and offered his hand to his old friend.

"Deal." Adam gripped his hand and tugged him in for a half-hug over the coffee table. Then he retreated to his desk. "Olivia, make a reservation for Eric Gaylord on the next flight to Nashville, Tennessee and call for a car to take him to the airport. Then book a flight for me." He lifted his finger off the button and the speaker cut out, only to cut back on.

"Where to, Mr. Parez?" Olivia asked.

"Home. I want to go home."

CHAPTER EIGHTEEN

"Hi, Mrs. Mortan." Dr. Hendricks gripped her hand in both of his in a gentle handshake then ushered her to a seat in his office.

"It's *Miss* Mortan," she replied shyly. Feeling like the town tramp, she fixed her eyes to the floor at her feet.

"Miss Mortan. May I ask a personal question?" Dr. Hendricks asked.

"Yes, of course."

"Do you plan on continuing with the pregnancy?"

She knew this was coming, but still it hurt. "Trust me, if I didn't have an abortion yet, I'm not going to." She dragged her eyes from the floor and met his gaze. "I'll be a good mother. Anything and everything my baby needs, it'll have. There's no other option to me than being the best mother I can be. I realize the baby will be born without a father, but I'll do my best." Her gaze dropped to the floor again. "I, uh, thought about adoption, but it's not for me."

Dr. Hendricks took out a prescription pad and started scribbling on it. "I only ask so I'll know how to properly care for you." He set the pen and pad down. "I've delivered many babies to families with both a mother and a father, and trust me when I say, it isn't always the best situation. Being a single mother has its challenges, but as long as you love your child, it makes it all worth it."

Lisa lifted her chin. "Thank you."

He smiled, his thick silver hair falling over his brow, and he smoothed it back. "Now, your job as a mother has already begun." He opened her chart. "Your blood pressure is elevated. Are you under any undue stress? Is the antique store proving too taxing on you?"

"How did you—"

He held up a hand. "Welcome to small town, Tennessee, my dear. You're not in New York anymore."

She snickered. "I see. Of course, I assume even in a small town, there is doctor-patient confidentiality?"

Dr. Hendricks smirked. "Yes, but I'll warn you. You don't want a small town gossip telling your business. That won't help your blood pressure at all. Trust me."

"I understand." Lisa clutched her purse tight to her chest. "If that's all, I'm needed at the shop."

"Not so fast." He ripped the slip from his prescription pad and handed it to her. "You need to take one prenatal vitamin daily. Have you been nauseous?"

"Only a little in the morning and evening," she said, taking the slip and tucking it into her purse. "It's actually been better since I moved here."

"Good. Are you sleeping and eating properly?"

Lisa wrung the shoulder strap of her purse. "I try,

but I'm not hungry most of the time."

"I'm guessing stress is playing a part in that, too. You need to eat five small meals a day. And it's important that you avoid stress as much as possible. Are you tired?"

"Only all the time." She smiled. "I fell asleep in the backroom during my break yesterday."

Dr. Hendricks smiled knowingly. "Wait here and I'll go check on your lab work." He pushed his castered chair back then meandered around the large wooden desk and left the office.

Her phone buzzed and she let go of the death grip on her purse to retrieve it. Judy's name appeared at the top of the display.

Need an item picked up at Nelson's thrift store, the text read. *Would you mind?*

Can do, Lisa replied.

The door opened behind her and she slid the phone back into her purse. "Everything okay, Dr. Hendricks?"

"Nothing to be worried about," he said, returning to his chair. "As I expected, your iron is a little low. I want to have you come back in two weeks to check it again. If it doesn't improve with your eating then I'll prescribe some iron pills."

"Oh, okay. Is that bad?"

"According to most of my patients, it isn't fun. The pills tend to cause upset stomach and constipation, so start eating."

"Yes, sir." Lisa gave a mock salute. "Anything else?" She scooted to the end of her chair and rose, offering her hand.

"One more thing. Here's a copy of your babies' sonogram."

"*Babies*?" She dropped her hand and stepped back, confused.

"Yes," Dr. Hendricks smiled. "There are two heart beats."

CHAPTER NINETEEN

Lisa's pulse didn't slow until she drove across the Sweetwater Creek Bridge into the lower income side of town, and pulled into a parking space in front of Nelson's thrift shop. She cut off the engine and gripped the steering wheel, taking a long breath.

Twins?

Seriously?

One baby scared her to death, but two? She couldn't even comprehend it. Two sets of clothes, two late night feedings, two of everything. What was everything anyway? She hadn't a clue what a baby needed. All she knew was what she'd seen on commercials, advertising a hundred and one different types of bottles or diapers.

She was sure she'd burst into tears, but instead she lowered her head to the wheel and concentrated on breathing. Maybe Mark was right. Maybe she really didn't have any business raising children. Wouldn't a mother know what her baby needed? Wanted? Heck, wouldn't a mother know she was carrying two babies, without needing a doctor to tell her? She'd been so stubborn she never believed anything Mark said was true, but he was right about one thing. She had no motherly instinct.

Leaning back, she rubbed her tummy. "Don't worry. I can't terminate you." Her heart ached to keep them, but how could she? There'd be two babies and only one of her.

Her phone trilled and she lifted it from the console next to her.

Eric's number.

Hi beautiful, the text read. *Can't wait to see you. Don't forget you're mine Friday night.*

Her body went numb. There was nothing else to do but tell him the truth when he returned. She nearly typed *you'll change your mind*, but decided it was best to keep the charade going. That was all it was between them anyway, some storybook fling that never had a chance to begin with.

Looking forward to it, she typed instead

It wasn't a complete lie. There was nothing more she wanted than to fall into his strong arms and sleep with him by her side all night, but that would never happen once she told him the truth, and now that truth was even bigger than it'd been a few minutes ago.

Two more days. Two more days and Eric would be out of her life. The doctor said she needed to come clean and avoid stress. She just had to make it until Friday then endure the rest of her life without him.

Visions of Mark throwing his wine glass across the room, red liquid dripping down his white walls and onto his immaculate carpet, flashed through her mind.

A sting coated her skin. The shards had come so close to hitting her.

Shoving the car door open, she brushed her thumb over the picture of Judy, Eric, and herself that she'd uploaded as her screen saver the day of the grand opening. What could've been, but will never be, haunted her.

The front door of the thrift store flew open and a shoulder plowed into her chest. Her feet flew out from under her and she crashed to the hard, icy front walk. Her right elbow and knee stung from impact.

"Hey! Watch where you're going," Cathy Mitchell barked, collapsing against the shop's door and grabbing the handle to keep herself upright.

A receipt floated to the slushy ground beside Lisa. She rolled over and rubbed her elbow before rising up to one knee.

Mrs. Mitchell hotfooted it toward her car.

Lisa grabbed the receipt and glanced down at it. Two chairs and a painting, sold to the thrift store, and for only pennies. "Hey, wait! Mrs. Mitchell, you forgot your receipt." Lisa finally managed to pull herself upright and held out the receipt while rubbing her low back to relieve the throbbing.

Mrs. Mitchell stormed back toward her like a wild boar, or whatever wild animals they had around here. "You had no right to look at that," she huffed, swiping her bangs out of her eyes before lifting her chin. "It's just charity, you know. I'm practically giving it away."

"Yes, I know. I saw the receipt. Why don't you let Judy and I sell it on consignment? You'll get a lot more for it."

"I don't need the money," she snapped. "Please, my husband left me a fortune. I practically own this whole town." She waved her hand dismissively before she leaned in. "Now, you don't need to go mentioning this to Judy or anyone else, got it? There's nothing to tell here, you understand?" Mrs. Mitchell waggled her finger at Lisa.

"You don't have anything to worry about. Apparently, I'm great at keeping secrets. But listen, I know you don't need the money, but if you want to sell merchandise and donate the funds to charity, why not let me sell them at the store?"

"Because I don't need that sassy Ms. Hotpants getting into my business. She knows every item I own, so she'll know right away if I have something in your store. And her sticky fingers would snatch it up in two shakes of a dog's tail. She already bought my candle sticks, you know."

"There's no reason she has to know. I'll tell you what, I can come by and take photos of the merchandise and sell them online. I've been working on adding an online version of the store. I won't advertise it locally, so she'll never even know about it. That way, you can sell whatever you'd like without the town knowing your business. How does that sound?"

Mrs. Mitchell thought for a moment. "Well, I guess. I mean, I should try for the best price, so I can donate more to charity, but this way I don't have to worry about Ms. Hotpants stealing my goods." Her face brightened as she straightened her knit cap and brushed some remaining ice flakes from her flaming-red coat. "By the way, you okay? You look a little run down, dear. If you hope to snag the most eligible bachelor in Sweetwater County, you best fix yourself up before he gets back into town."

Lisa forced a smile. "Thanks, I will." She didn't have to look in a mirror to know her face had gotten thin over the past couple of weeks and her belly a little larger. With twins, she'd probably be as big as that town car Mrs. Mitchell drove before she even reached her third trimester. Heck, she didn't even know what a trimester was until Dr. Hendricks handed her the pregnancy brochure. Geesh, this was all too crazy.

Lisa nodded farewell to Mrs. Mitchell then yanked the thrift store door open, her back protesting the movement, and ambled inside, every step taxing on her legs.

Just inside, a double stroller stood on display. Her hands shook at the site. It was enormous. How did it even fit through the aisles of a store? It certainly wouldn't fit through the narrow walkways of the antique shop. The store she needed to be working at right now, but she didn't want to face Judy. Not now. She needed to process the news she'd just learned before she could share it with anyone else.

Of course, it would take her until the twins went to college before she could process all of this craziness.

CHAPTER TWENTY

Horns blared in competition, as if they'd move the cars crawling through the Paris streets forward faster. The noise agitated Eric, taking him back to his life in New York City. He didn't know when it happened, but Sweetwater County, Tennessee, and its quiet country atmosphere, was where his heart lived. Perhaps it always had.

Watching the droplets of rain meander down the side window of the cab, he eyed the blurred sites of the *City of Love* one last time. In the grey morning light, the romantic city had altered into a hustling mess, full of fast-paced deals, tourists, and people on the go.

He fisted his hands, willing the cab to go faster. He'd missed the flight the night before. This was his only shot to get home today, without making four transfers.

Slipping his phone from his pocket, he checked for messages, but found none. Scrolling through his Paris photos from the one night he'd walked around the city, he spotted the picture of his mother, Lisa, and himself at the store opening. Light shone on Lisa's hair, making her look like an angel. God, that woman was beautiful. More beautiful than any he'd seen. Her bright smile, large doe eyes, and high cheekbones mesmerized him.

"Hey, monsieur, what airline?" the cabbie shouted in a heavy French accent back through the slit in the window.

"Air France," Eric hollered back, before slipping his phone back in his pocket and pulling the last of his Euros from his wallet.

The cab rolled to a stop, and he handed the money to the cabbie, the burly man's face nearly hidden behind a thick beard. "Keep the change. Thanks." He didn't wait for the man to reach the back before he bolted from the cab, yanked the trunk open, and retrieved his suitcase. The air was full of exhaust fumes, instead of the welcoming smell of fresh baked bread that filled the streets in town.

"Have safe flight," the man called out.

Eric waved. "Thanks," he said, before he raced through the automatic doors to the check-in desk.

Once his bag was safely tucked behind the counter, he made his way to the security checkpoint. Stuck in the long line, he kept glancing at his watch. There was still time, but for some reason he just couldn't wait another day to get home.

A young woman lifted her baby from a stroller as she neared security. Swaddling her infant close, she pushed the stroller ahead, catching it on the corner of an upturned mat. The young child cooed and giggled, thrusting himself high on her shoulder. The little eyes caught Eric's attention. His heart tightened at the sight of the small mouth and two tiny teeth smiling at him.

He stepped away, as if the child carried some sort of disease. It was the closest he'd been to a baby since he'd learned of his own unborn child's death.

Taking a deep breath, he eased closer. "Let me help, ma'am."

She switched her child to her other shoulder, the little hand reaching for Eric's hair. "No, no," she chided the boy. She gently guided the little arm back down with her hand. "Sorry, he's into the hair pulling stage, you know," she said to Eric.

No. He didn't know.

"Thanks so much." The woman smiled warmly. "My husband flew home ahead of me, and I've had a rough time on my own. You're the first kind person I've run into so far, so I thank you."

"It's no problem." Eric looked at the security guard, who took the stroller from him. Then he set his bag on the belt, his watch and cell phone in a small basket. "I'm sure it must be difficult traveling alone with a baby," he managed before she walked through the metal detector.

Another security guard waved him through and he retrieved his belongings. "You must be a great dad," she mumbled before snuggling her baby back into the stroller.

The darkness he'd managed to escape for the last couple of weeks shot through him once more. The innocence and delicate nature of the child sitting before him shredded his newfound happiness. A child needed protection and love. He'd given his neither. "I don't know about that," he said under his breath.

"What's that?" the young woman asked. "I'm sorry, I couldn't hear you over his squeals." She pointed to her son.

"Nothing. You have a great flight." He tipped his head, grabbed his bag and slipped his shoes back on. He concentrated on every motion, as if there was no room in his mind or soul for anything but the monotonous movement of a traveler.

His phone buzzed in his hand and he glanced down. Two missed calls, both from his mother.

Once he reached his terminal, he retreated to a lone corner, away from everyone, and dialed his mother. The phone rang once then clicked and rang a few more times.

"Eric, hon. How are you?" His mother's voice boosted his spirits. She had that infectious gift of happiness.

"I'm fine, Mom. How are you?" Eric asked.

"Um, better than you by the way it sounds." His mother's concerned tone penetrated the long distance.

"I'm on my way home." He changed his own tone to mask his sadness. "I should be home by tomorrow afternoon. I've got a layover in Atlanta, but I'm on my way."

"That's great news," she squealed. "I've missed you, and I'm not the only one. I hear you and Lisa have gotten to know each other better."

"Yes, Mom. And you were right. We do have a lot in common. It's time for me to come home and tell her about my past. If she still wants a man who could abandon her, then I'm willing to move forward."

"If you're not ready, it's fine. But if you are, then let the past go."

"Believe it or not, I had. It's just..." he glanced around, "I saw a baby today and well, it was difficult." Eric rubbed his chest with the palm of his hand, trying to loosen the tightness. "I'm ready to start dating someone. I'll always remember what happened, but I've forgiven myself for Mary Lynn. The baby part is a little more difficult, but hey, I don't have to deal with that yet. And I think Lisa will be understanding and not mind taking things slow. Perhaps someday I'll want to have a child, but right now, I still feel like I'd make an inadequate father. I guess you were right about that, too. Everything happens for a reason. God's giving me a chance to find love and heal slowly before I move forward, and I'm ready to do that."

Silence filled the line.

"Mom? You still there?"

"Yes," she said, her voice sounding further away than before. "Eric?"

"Yeah?"

"I think you should come see me first, before you go to Lisa."

"Boarding flight 876 to Atlanta, Georgia, USA," the announcer called over the PA. "Boarding flight 876 to Atlanta, Georgia, USA."

"Sure, I'll come straight to the store to see you. But I've got to go now. They're boarding. Love you."

"I love you, too, son."

He hit *end* and ambled to the boarding line.

Finally, he was going home. He'd hold Lisa in his arms, and something inside told him she could heal his heart, and he'd heal her right back. They were brought together, like his mom said, and things could go slow, and they would just be together.

The tightness in his chest faded as he walked down the gangway. For the first time in several years, happiness drove the darkness away. Yes, he was ready to be with Lisa. For once in his life, everything seemed to be working out.

CHAPTER TWENTY-ONE

Lisa stood in the center of her living room, eyeing the sharp-cornered glass-topped coffee table, the hardwood floors, exposed outlets, glass figurines, and other dangerous objects. A toddler wouldn't last a week in her home. She sighed, glancing at the empty boxes stacked in the corner.

All night she'd prayed it had all been a dream, that the doctor had made a mistake, or that the entire pregnancy never even happened. Her head and body ached from crying and begging God to help. But it was all true, and if she was going to be a mother, it wasn't about her anymore. She'd tell Eric the truth and move on with her life, focusing on the babies.

She gathered several odds and ends that were heavy and breakable and placed them on the glass table. Good thing she worked in an antique store. She'd need some new furniture. Standing at her picture window, she took in the landscape. Not a bad place to raise children, with the trees, open land, and friendly people.

Knock. Knock.

Lisa drew her gaze from the sunrise peeking over the mountain in the distance and went to her front door. She eyed a deliveryman on her porch, holding a beautiful floral arrangement in front of his face, then reluctantly turned the lock and opened the door.

"Good morning, ma'am." His thick, southern accent eased her tension.

"Good morning. Are those for me?"

"Are you Ms. Mortan?" he asked.

"Yes."

"Then, yes. They're for you." When he lowered the flowers, offering them to her, she got her first glimpse at his crooked teeth and scruffy face, but his smile was endearing. "The gentleman who ordered these was adamant you receive them before work this morning." He shuffled between feet.

"Really? Well, thank you. Oh, wait here a second." Lisa snatched her purse from the table in the entryway. "Here." Lisa took the flowers from him and he took his tip. "Thanks again." With the glass vase heavy in her arms, she kicked the front door closed and made her way to the kitchen table.

The scent of fresh lilacs filled the room with a pleasant, sweet aroma. A small envelope protruded from the end of a long clear plastic fork, addressed to *Beautiful*.

Sliding her finger under the sealed paper, it popped free and she pulled the card out.

I can't wait to see you. It's time for us to move forward. After all the talks we've had and time we've spent together, I'm ready to tell you everything, and

I'm ready to listen. I know we'll only be closer. Trust me with your heart. I won't break it. Eric.

A tear slipped down her cheek. If only he knew the truth and still wanted her. No man could ever love a woman carrying another man's baby, no, two babies. Or could he?

The front door flew open and wind gusted through the hallway into the kitchen, chilling her to the core. She raced to the entryway. When she rounded the corner, a man in a suit was standing in the doorway. Not just any man. Mark, and he looked angrier than she'd ever seen him before.

"You told me you terminated the fetus," he growled. He crossed the threshold, his fists clutched at his side.

She instinctively wrapped her arms around her belly. "Listen, I don't know how you found out—"

"You're not real bright, are you? Where do you think the insurance company sent the doctor bill?"

Silently, she cursed herself for such an epic mistake. After forwarding her mail to the shop, changing her address for every credit card and bank account, she'd forgotten about updating her health insurance. "You don't have to worry. I don't want anything from you." Backing into the sitting room, she rounded into the kitchen and snatched her car keys from the counter. The familiar furrowed dark brow, pressed lips and twitching jaw warned her to protect her unborn children. He'd only grabbed her arm last time, but she didn't want to find out how far he'd take it this time.

He advanced and she cowered away from him, trying to put the dining table between them.

Mark sighed, running his hand through his hair, and retreated to the sofa. "I'm sorry I grabbed you. Don't run. We need to talk." He glanced at her, his face softer but still accusing. "You lied to me."

"I couldn't terminate—"

"Not just about that," he shouted, "about everything. We had an arrangement. Neither of us wanted children, ever. Remember? We are not fit to be parents."

Lisa took a cautious step toward him. "I didn't mean for this to happen, Mark. And I agree that we weren't meant to be parents. That's why I came here. I wanted to find a good home for our child."

Mark shot up. "No. The system doesn't work." He lifted his sleeve. "You know how awful it is in foster care." He pointed to the faded cigarette burns on his forearm. "You see this? It's what a foster dad does when you don't take out the trash." He yanked down the collar of his expensive shirt, popping off one of the buttons. "This is what happens when you fall asleep watching television." More burn marks dotted his neck and collarbone.

"I knew how you felt about foster care, that's why I was finding a family to adopt the baby."

"Adoption's no better. No. I won't put a child through that. You have to terminate. And I'm here to make sure you do."

"I don't understand. You'll give millions to children's charities, but you want to kill your own child?"

Mark advanced. "That's different. Those children are already here. We don't have to add to the problem. Why are you making this so difficult? Just end the pregnancy and then we'll both be free."

"Free? Is that all you care about?" Lisa shouted at him for the first time in the two years they'd been together.

He stopped, his eyes wide, and his mouth dropped for a second before he recovered. "You're not going to trap me like my mother did my father. I'm not going to work myself into an early grave just to have you toss that child out when the money stops. I won't do it." His lip curled into a snarl.

"And I won't ask you to. I promise, I won't," she said, standing her ground. "I'll keep the baby and I won't ask for a dime. I'm not your mother."

"Liar." He advanced again, his jaw tight, his face crimson.

This wasn't going to end like last time. With his extra foot of height and twice her weight, she knew that, at best, she'd walk away with a few bruises. But at the worst, the babies would be harmed.

Mark lunged and snatched her arm. "Give me the keys," he snarled. "You're not going anywhere but to an abortion clinic."

Obediently, she dropped the keys on the floor. When he bent down to retrieve them, she snatched the bowl of fruit off the counter and crashed it over his head. Then she bolted from the kitchen, down the hall, and out the front door. With no cell phone, coat, or shoes, she raced through the neighbor's yard and down the back alley to the main street.

Every inch of her body shook with fear and cold. Her feet crushed something sharp. Glancing down, she spotted blood on her toes, but still she didn't stop. Her legs continued to move, as if by their own will. She pumped her arms and sprinted between bushes. Crossing the next street, cars squealed to a halt, but she just kept running. With no real direction, only one word pounded in her head. *Protect*.

Lisa halted at an intersection and looked behind her. There was no sign of Mark. Oh, God. Did she seriously injure him? Had she overreacted?

A familiar car rolled to a stop in front of her and she stumbled back with a gasp.

"Darling, what are you doing out here dressed like that?" Cathy Mitchell leaned over the passenger's seat. "You're going to catch your death. Get in."

Another car turned onto the street, the luxury vehicle sticking out amongst the dirty trucks and SUVs lining the curbs. Lisa hopped in the car.

"What's going on, dear?" Mrs. Mitchell asked. "You look like you've seen a ghost."

Lisa swung around, peering through the back window. Mark's car was getting closer. "Drive. Just drive."

Mrs. Mitchell grasped the steering wheel. "All righty, hon. Calm yourself. Where to?"

"I...I don't know. Just drive." Lisa wrung her hands and turned back to face the front. "To the store. To main street. There's lots of people there."

"Okay, dear." Mrs. Mitchell slid the gearshift into drive then turned the corner, heading to Main Street.

"Hurry. Please," Lisa begged, catching a glimpse of Mark's car in the side mirror.

"You want me to step on it?" Mrs. Mitchell shot her a sideways smirk.

"Yes."

Mrs. Mitchell smashed the pedal to the floor and they flew through multiple side streets, cars slamming on their brakes to avoiding hitting them. The woman belonged in movies as a stunt car driver. They took a turn so sharply Lisa thought two wheels would come off the ground.

"I'm sorry I got you involved in this," Lisa muttered.

"Oh, dear. Don't be. I needed a little excitement. Besides, don't you know? I like to be in the middle of everything." Mrs. Mitchell winked then cornered sharply again at the bakery before squealing to a stop in front of the antique store. "You'll be safe here." She slid her cell phone from her pocket and started dialing. "Go on inside and get yourself cleaned up."

"What about you?" Lisa asked, swinging around to keep an eye out for Mark.

"Don't worry, we lost him. Oh, and I'll be fine. Trust me." Mrs. Mitchell shooed her out the car.

Lisa gave her the best smile she could manage. "Thanks," she said, but the woman was already lost in her phone call, no doubt recounting Lisa's strange behavior and whatever gossip she wanted to share. Lisa sighed. It was time. The truth needed to be told before gossip could spread. That was what Dr. Hendricks and Judy had encouraged her to do.

Maneuvering out of the car, her feet burned in protest. Her back ached and her stomach cramped. She mounted the few steps to the front door before she saw Mark's car turn onto Main Street. Her gut clenched tight as she hurried into the store. She needed a moment to think, to figure out what to do.

The bell jingled above the door and Judy appeared by the register. Lisa's belly knotted tight and the pressure down low became so intense she thought her insides would fall out. She took two steps then spasms clenched her back tight. Crying out, she fell to the floor.

"Eric!" Judy yelled.

Eric?

Through the pain ripping her pelvis apart, she heard footsteps shuffl into the main room. Blood pooled around Lisa's knees and she doubled over, tears pouring down her face. "Oh, God. No."

A commotion sounded outside. The door swung open and she caught a glimpse of red and purple. "The store's closed," Mrs. Mitchell's voice carried inside before it shut again.

"It'll be okay." Judy wrapped her motherly arms around Lisa and rocked her. "Eric, call an ambulance."

"Eric?" Lisa looked up through tear-filled eyes. "I'm sorry. Please don't hate me," she murmured.

"I know she's in there," Mark's voice burst through the seams around the door, threatening to invade.

Another cramp twisted her belly in knots, taking her breath away, and she gasped.

Eric dropped to his knees and wiped the tears from her face. "Never. I don't know what's going on, but I'll do whatever I can to make it better."

Lisa fought her constricting throat to form words. "I'm pregnant, Eric. That's what I wanted to tell you. At least...I was."

CHAPTER TWENTY-TWO

His mother rubbed his shoulder. "Honey, I'm so sorry."

"I can't...I can't do this. Not again." He bolted for the bathroom. "This isn't happening." Leaning on the sink, he concentrated on slowing his pulse and taking long, steady breaths before he faced himself in the mirror. His bloodshot eyes stared back at him. He wanted to scream, to yell at God and tell him it wasn't fair. None of it.

The look on Lisa's face, the terror reflected in her beautiful eyes. How did he not know she was pregnant? How stupid he'd been. Yet, his mother, she'd known the entire time.

He yanked off his tie and shoved it in his pocket before splashing water on his face. His hands continued to tremble. "Give me strength," he pleaded.

Lisa faced losing a child. Had she told the father about the baby, or had she run off. Had she done the same thing that Mary Lynn had done to him?

His anguish subsided and anger gripped his soul.

Slamming his palms against the countertop, he straightened and headed back to the waiting room. If she didn't lose the baby, the father had a right to know. And when he did, he'd step up and be a part of her life, of the baby's life.

Halfway down the hall, he spotted a woman with a black eye in the waiting room, and remembered the bruise on Lisa's wrist. What if she'd fled because the father was abusive? If so, then did the father still have a right to know about his child? *Yes*, Eric told himself. Every man deserved to see their child.

"Eric." His mother held up her hands, cutting him off from the waiting room. "You don't know everything."

"Does the father know about the baby?" Eric asked, his cool tone causing him to swallow down his anger.

"Yes, but there's always more to the story." His mother squeezed both his arms. "The father's at the nurse's station now. But, he's not like you, Eric. Not all men want to be a father."

Eric stepped back, scanning the room. "He's here?"

"Yes." His mother dropped her hands to her side.

"Then he cares. He'll want to be a part of the baby's life." He swallowed down the darkness that wormed its way back through his body. He'd lost a woman he loved and a baby he didn't know about, all in one day. "History repeats itself," he muttered.

His mother grabbed his hand. "No, it hasn't. This isn't the same. Lisa isn't Mary Lynn and it wasn't your baby. We don't even know yet if Lisa lost the child."

A nurse in surgical scrubs approached them. "Mrs.

Gaylord? Lisa would like to see you."

"Come." His mother waved him to follow.

As if his feet had a mind of their own, they shuffled forward, his body following without the energy to protest. The numbness had already returned to his soul.

Taking the elevator to the sixth floor, they exited onto the maternity ward and saw a man pacing around the nurse's station. A look of pure terror radiated from him. Eric knew that look, the look of losing his child.

"Don't do it, Eric," his mother whispered. "Come and see Lisa with me. She'll want to explain."

But Eric just shook his head and released his mother's hand. He approached the man who stopped pacing and turned to the nurse's station. "Listen, I give permission to terminate the pregnancy."

Eric froze. The man must really love Lisa if he was willing to make a tough decision like that. *And where does that leave me?*

"Sir, you have no legal rights to make that decision," the nurse said. "You're not married to Ms. Mortan."

"Then I want to speak to her. Now."

"Ms. Mortan is in a delicate state right now. Tests are still being run. You should return to the waiting room until Ms. Mortan sends for you." The nurse gestured down the hallway toward the waiting room.

He scrubbed his face, small cuts marring the backs of his hands. "Why does that woman get to go in and see her, but I can't?" the man demanded, pointing at Eric's mother.

"Because Ms. Mortan requested her."

The man slammed his fist down on the counter then turned in a huff. A doctor approached cautiously, nodding to the stunned nurse behind the desk and the nurse reached for the phone.

The doctor cut the man off as he advanced toward Lisa's room. "Sir, if you don't calm down, I'll have security remove you from the premises."

Eric straightened and nudged his mother toward Lisa's room before approaching the man, not sure if he wanted to slug the guy or take him for a drink. "Hi, I'm Eric Gaylord."

Both the doctor and the man turned. "So?" the man retorted.

"I understand you're the father of Lisa's baby?" Eric asked, clenching his fist at the man's arrogant attitude. This was the same man he'd seen in the articles he'd found online. The fiancé from New York.

The man rolled his eyes. "If it's even mine," he huffed. "That whore claims it's mine, but she also claimed she terminated the pregnancy before leaving New York."

Eric clenched and unclenched his hands, fighting back the urge to punch the guy for calling Lisa a whore. *The man's just upset*, he told himself. Putting his attorney mask on, he asked, "She told you she'd terminated the pregnancy?"

"Yeah, can you believe that? The bitch tells me that then leaves, so I think it's all done, nothing to worry about. Then some insurance carrier sends an obstetric bill from some bible squawking, backwards town in

Tennessee." The man glared at the closed door to Lisa's room. "Well, she's not going to get away with this."

Eric took a step forward, ignoring the tug of his mother's grip on his shirt. "Listen, I know you're upset, but you need to tone it down. I've been lied to as well. But trust me, if I had a chance to hold my baby in my arms I'd do anything to make it happen. I'm not sure what occurred between you two, but don't walk away. You've got a chance at a family."

"Family?" the man huffed. "What—" His phone buzzed and he held up one finger. "Mark here," he said, pressing the phone against his ear.

Eric's mother pulled on his arm, tugging him away from the man. "Not every man is like you, son," she whispered. "He might not stand up for Lisa. You don't know the entire story. Trust me when I say she did the best she could."

Eric watched the man pace, chuckle and speak into the phone.

"Yeah," the man said to the person on the other line. "I'm stuck in some backward ass town in the middle of nowhere." He paused, listening, then said, "Oh, she'll pay for this. I'll make sure she never works in New York again."

Eric shook his head. "No, he just needs time," he said to his mother. "He's in shock." He could remember all too well what that was like.

His mother squeezed his hand. "I hope you're right. But if not, are you going to let her go? You haven't smiled or laughed in years, not like you have since Lisa entered your life. You came back to see her, to tell her everything. That hasn't changed. You know her secret, now let her know yours."

"Mrs. Gaylord, she's ready for you," the doctor said and his mother disappeared through the door.

Eric rubbed his throbbing temple. The pain of her crying in his arms, the thought of her losing her baby, or dying herself, tore him up inside, but it wasn't his baby. He didn't need to relive it all again. It wasn't his business. He turned his back on the door and willed himself to walk out of the hospital, but his feet wouldn't move.

CHAPTER TWENTY-THREE

Stark white walls, stiff bedding, and the smell of disinfectant told Lisa she'd made it to the hospital. The room spun, but she fought to sit up.

"Stay still," Judy said. "The doctor gave you something to help with the pain and let you relax. You gave us quite a scare, you know."

"My...my babies?" Lisa cupped her hand over her belly. "How are—"

"We don't know anything yet," Judy said, gently pushing Lisa back down. "Don't worry. I had lots of bleeding with my pregnancy, too, and everything worked out just fine." Judy stopped and stared down at her. "Wait, babies?"

"Yes." Lisa could barely hear her own voice.

Knock. Knock.

"Yes?" Judy answered. "That should be the doctor now."

Dr. Hendricks and a nurse entered and approached her bed. "Ms. Mortan. How are you feeling?"

"Okay, I guess." Anticipation stung her skin and she wanted to blurt out for them to tell her about her babies.

There was another knock and the door opened again, long enough for her to catch a glimpse of Mark pacing around the nurse's station. "Has she lost it yet?" Mark's voice traveled in with the nurse carrying a chart.

"Here, Doctor," the nurse said, handing the chart to Dr. Hendricks.

Dr. Hendricks scanned the documents on the clipboard, flipping the pages back and forth. "I see you didn't heed my warning about avoiding stress."

Lisa shook her head. "Stress found me."

Dr. Hendricks gave her a sympathetic look. "I see. Well, I have the test results here. Would you like the father to be present?"

"No!" Lisa swallowed and sunk back into the bed. "No, thank you."

"Is it okay if I stay?" Judy squeezed Lisa's hand.

"Yes, please." Lisa held tight to Judy, terrified to discover the fate of her babies.

"Ms. Mortan, you went into preterm labor due to excessive stress," the doctor said slowly. "I'm afraid you've lost one of the babies." His words were harsh, but his voice soft, his eyes sympathetic.

"No," she gasped. But the shock quickly faded, replaced by grief and regret. "It's all my fault," she muttered, her voice breaking. "I...I didn't mean it. I wanted both babies. I swear. Oh, God what have I done?"

"You haven't done anything," Dr. Hendricks said,

laying a comforting hand on her shoulder. "It's twin gestation. Sometimes one baby is stronger than the other and this happens, but I'm afraid there's more." Dr. Hendricks took a long breath. "We're unsure about the health of the remaining fetus. There was excessive blood loss. We've been able to stop the bleeding, but it's imperative you avoid stress and remain on bed rest for the time being. Possibly for the remainder of your pregnancy."

"What do you mean? Is it also dead?" Lisa sobbed.

"No," the doctor assured her. "There's a heartbeat, but there's no guarantee the baby won't be born with some sort of issue, a mental or physical defect."

"I see." Lisa scooted down until she was lying on her back, staring up at the ceiling. *Punishment? Was that what this was?*

"I'll let you rest." Dr. Hendrickson squeezed her shoulder before he and his nurse backed away and disappeared from Lisa's blurred vision.

"It's not your fault," Judy whispered, stroking Lisa's hair from her forehead.

"Isn't it? I didn't want two babies. I hadn't even decided what I was going to do with one. Mark was right. I'll make a terrible mother."

"Says who?" Judy stopped stroking her hair and gave her a stern yet soft look. "Don't let anyone convince you of such nonsense, especially him. He's just being selfish. That man hurt you. The police will be in for a statement soon. Just you wait, he'll be out of your life for good," Judy stated.

"And then what?"

"Then you can move on with your life."

"How? As a single mother of a child with special needs?" Lisa shook her head. "I don't know if I can do this alone."

"Oh, hon." Judy rested her hand against Lisa's cheek. "You're not alone. You have me and Eric."

"Eric? You don't see him in here, do you? He knows the truth now. He realized how screwed up everything is and bolted." She sighed. "Honestly, I don't blame him."

"No, it's not like that," Judy protested.

"Then what is it like? He's out buying a cradle for some other man's baby?" The words rolled off Lisa's tongue before she could stop them. Judy didn't deserve her hatred. It wasn't meant for her.

"Listen, I know you're upset, but there are things about Eric you still don't know. Eric has his own troubles. He came home early from Europe so he could tell you. He's never spoken about it to anyone before as far as I know. That means something, doesn't it?"

"Then tell me why he isn't here," Lisa demanded.

"I can't. That's for him to say." Judy stiffened, her arms like mechanical robots as she poured water from a plastic pitcher into a cup before offering it to Lisa.

Lisa took a sip from the straw, the cool liquid coating her sore throat, then collapsed back into the pillows. She'd done this. Caused all this pain and suffering in people she'd already grown to appreciate, possibly even love. But it wasn't just her. It was Mark. He'd been a big part of the death of her baby.

Hatred she'd never felt before wiggled up her back

like a serpent of pure anger. "Can you call the sheriff, please? I want to make a statement and be done with this. All of it." She clenched the sheet. She needed to put her life in order for the sake of the baby that had survived, and the first place to start was with Mark. He needed to be gone, for good.

Judy snuck out of the room without another word and returned with the sheriff.

"Hello, ma'am," the sheriff greeted her, tipping his hat. "I'm ready to take your statement."

"Great." Lisa bowed her head, grinding her teeth with the knowledge she'd done this to herself. How did she become the one thing she promised never to be? A battered woman.

"Can you tell me what happened this morning when Mr. Brenson arrived at your residence?'"

Lisa lifted her chin. "He came in the front door, uninvited, and told me he'd found out I was still pregnant. He wanted to know why I hadn't terminated the pregnancy."

"Did he believe you were going to?" the sheriff asked.

"Yes. I told him I'd already taken care of it before I left New York," Lisa answered.

"I see. What happened after that?"

"He was angry. I grabbed my keys from the kitchen counter and tried to leave, but he grabbed me and I dropped the keys. When he bent down to pick them up, I smashed a bowl over his head before fleeing out the front door."

"You were found without any shoes on, your foot

bleeding. Did he attack you as you were leaving?"

"No. I ran. I didn't want to take a chance on him catching me. I didn't know what he'd do. I thought he'd harm my babies." She swallowed, forcing down the scream of despair that tried to escape. "Turns out he did."

"So, he never physically assaulted you, but you hit him over the head with a bowl which required stitches?" the officer asked.

Stitches? Good. It served him right for wanting to hurt her babies.

Judy rounded the bed. "Now, wait just a minute. That man intended harm, and you and I both know it. She did the smart thing and fought back, long enough to escape. Yet, you make it sound like she's the abuser. Now, you listen here, little Jimmy Mason—"

"It's Sheriff Mason," he corrected, his face turning red.

"I used to babysit you when you were a little thing," Judy retorted, "and if you're gonna act like a naïve little boy, I'm gonna treat you like one." Judy's accent thickened the angrier she became.

"He's right," Lisa said. "Mark isn't stupid. He's got money and influence. He'll get away with everything." Her insides twisted at her realization that she'd never win.

"Listen, I don't want to upset you right now," the sheriff said, "but Mr. Brenson states he won't press charges if he's allowed to speak to you."

"What?" Judy said. "Have you lost your mind, Jimmy? That man is obviously upset and you want to let him see her? Did the doctor forget to mention how she's supposed to avoid stress?"

Lisa bit back a frustrated laugh. Mark held all the cards, just like he always did. But this time she wouldn't let him stack the deck. One way or another, that man would be out of her life for good. He was right about one thing. He could never be a father. "It's okay," she said. "I'll speak to him. I need to face him, tell him the truth, and there isn't a safer place than this. Besides, I don't want to give birth to my baby in a jail cell."

"Do you want me to stay, dear?" Judy rubbed her arm.

"No, this is something I need to do alone."

"Okay, we'll be right outside. Right, *Sheriff*?"

"Yes, ma'am. All you need to do, Ms. Mortan, is shout and we'll be in quick."

"Thank you."

Judy shuffled to the door and waved Mark over. "You upset her and I'll do a lot worse than cause a few stitches."

"Are you sure that's a good idea?" Eric's voice floated into the room from the hall, like a firefly illuminating Lisa's way to a happier place, but then Mark stepped inside and the light immediately vanished, leaving her heart in darkness.

Mark waited for the door to shut before he approached.

Lisa stiffened, but refused to allow him to cause her surviving baby any more stress. "What do you want?"

"You know what I want." He stood rigid by her bed, looking up and down the length of her. "Weak. Just like your crack whore of a mother. You couldn't even keep both babies. Why do you think you'll be strong enough to care for the one that survived? Especially one that's deformed."

"The baby is not deformed," she said through clenched teeth. "And even if it does have challenges, I'll be there to help. You don't have to worry about the money. I don't want anything from you."

The machine beside her bed beeped. She didn't have to look to know her blood pressure was rising. The heat on her cheeks and her tingling fingertips was evidence enough.

"That's what they all say." His eyes flickered to the window, a distant look casting over his dark features. His jaw loosened, and his Adams Apple rose up then down. Fear. That was what she saw in his eyes.

Lisa straightened in the bed. "What are you so scared of?"

"I'm not scared of anything." His face morphed back into the stone cold, hard-lined lips and furrowed brow she was so used to.

"I'm not sure what's going on, but this isn't a repeat of what happened with your parents. This baby will not be placed in an abusive foster home. I won't let that happen. I'm stronger than you think I am."

He stepped closer, glaring down at her. "And I won't let you trap me. I've already demanded a DNA test be performed. I know you were whoring around on me."

Lisa gasped. "Never."

"You think I'll believe you? After the lies you told me in New York," he said, his voice growing louder.

Hearing the machine beep again, Lisa took a deep breath to calm herself. "If you're so sure it's not yours, then why are you so insistent I terminate?"

He gaped at her a moment, but before he could form words Dr. Hendricks shuffled into the room.

"Mr. Brenson, I'm afraid I can't authorize a test to determine the baby's DNA at this time," the doctor said, his usual jolly bedside manner lost for the moment. Glancing beyond him, she spotted Judy and Eric in the doorway. Her heart thundered at the sight of them both. The embarrassment at her situation made her want to crawl under the sheets and never come out.

"Ms. Mortan is too high risk. Perhaps in a few weeks, or possibly not until the baby is born."

"Born? That'll be months." Mark spun around to face the doctor.

"That's normal biology, yes," Dr. Hendricks joked.

Mark advanced on him. "You think this is humorous? I'm being trapped by some second rate, sorry excuse for a whore and you're making jokes?"

Eric stomped to the doctor's side. "It's time for you to leave," he snarled, the calm, endearingly handsome man not his usual friendly self. Instead, he puffed out his chest and dared Mark to cross him.

"Ms. Mortan cannot handle any more stress," Dr. Hendricks explained, "and I'm afraid the monitors are indicating you are a stressor. So we'll need you to leave her room for now."

To emphasize the doctor's point, Sheriff Mason rounded the corner, his arms crossed. "I believe you need some time to calm down, son."

Before Mark could respond, Mrs. Mitchell entered, flamboyant in a purple and red hat. The hospital room was becoming a public display of Lisa's epic failure in bedding a man who wanted his own child dead.

"It's you!" Mark snapped at Mrs. Mitchell. "What're you doing here? I thought you said you and the other purple hat, crazy blue hairs were having some secret meeting in the antique store?"

Mrs. Mitchell blinked then waved her gloved hand at him. "Oh, honey, we're just a bunch of old senile ladies who can't get the date right. Turns out our meeting is next Tuesday."

Mark growled then turned on Lisa. "Is this what you want? To live in this freak show of a town?" He stormed out of the room, leaving her to deal with the looks of disgust on everyone's faces.

Sheriff Mason followed him out, with Eric close behind.

Mrs. Mitchell gave her triumphant smile, as if she'd exiled an evil villain and saved the damsel in distress. She meant well, and Lisa was thankful for any help in ridding her life of Mark Brenson. She returned the smile and watched the woman march from the room, the red plume atop of her hat fluttering in the air.

"Rest," Dr. Hendricks told her. "The nurse will be in shortly to give you something to help you sleep." Then the doctor left, too.

"I'm sorry about that," Lisa said to Judy, rubbing her temple, and the IV cord caught on the bed rail. Her entire world was spinning out of control and she was stuck in bed, trying not to get upset.

"Let me help you with that, dear," Judy said, coming to her side.

Eric stuck his head in. "Can I come in for a moment?"

Lisa nodded, but part of her didn't want him to come in. She knew he was too much of a gentleman to flee without a word, despite what he'd said. He wasn't Mark, but he was still human. No one would stick around for this insanity.

Judy snatched her bag from the tray beside Lisa's bed. "Well, I need to go take care of a few things. Can you stay with Lisa until I get back?"

"Of course," Eric said.

Judy kissed Lisa's forehead. "Get some rest, dear."

As Judy disappeared from the room and Eric closed the door behind his mother, Lisa kept her gaze on the thin white blanket stretched over her legs. She heard his heavy footsteps cross the room then Eric placed a finger under her chin and tugged her face up to look at him.

"Hey, now. I'm here as a friend, not a judge and jury."

She opened her mouth to speak, but couldn't manage a single word, so she closed it again. She wanted to tell him how sorry she was, or how she wished things were different, or that he deserved so much better than being dragged into her mess. She hoped he didn't hate her, but none of those words escaped. When she finally cleared her throat and managed to speak, all she could say was, "I lost a baby."

He nodded then lowered the arm of the bed and sat beside her on the edge of the thin mattress. "I heard. I'm sorry."

"It's my fault," she choked.

"No. It's not. Don't blame yourself." When he took her into his arms, the tears flowed. "Shh." He rocked her gently, kissing her head.

"I know you must hate me," she sobbed into his chest.

"No. Never." Eric tightened his hug. "I'm so sorry." His voice cracked.

Footsteps entered the room then coldness flooded up her arm. She didn't have to see the nurse to know she'd been given something through her IV.

When the sobbing slowed, he grabbed tissues from the table and leaned her back against the pillow. "Rest. You're exhausted. I'll be here when you wake up."

"You don't have to be. I can do this on my own," she mumbled, but her eyes fluttered, trying to stay open. She caught his concerned gaze, saw his eyes full of tears.

His hand brushed strands of hair from her moist cheek. "I can't believe it's happening again," he muttered. "But this time I'll do the right thing."

"What?" Lisa managed before darkness won.

CHAPTER TWENTY-FOUR

Eric held her against him as she slept. The warmth of her body made him feel connected to someone for the first time in years, like they could handle anything together. They weren't together, though. Mark was the father and he was right outside in the hallway.

He leaned to the side, slipping his phone from his pocket while trying not to wake her. It wasn't his place to get involved, but the lawyer inside of him urged him to look into Mark's background.

Searching Google, he didn't find anything more on the man than he'd learned when he was researching Lisa, just that Mark Brenson was a well-to-do philanthropist in New York. If the man didn't own something, then he donated to it, indicating he had power and influence. So then, why didn't he have an attorney represent him, instead of driving all the way out here? Perhaps he did care for Lisa, but his ego wouldn't let him show his true feelings in front of all these people.

Eric set the phone down on his lap and watched the clear liquid drop into the tube leading to Lisa's arm.

Even as she slept her brow was still furrowed. She'd face so much grief every day for the rest of her life. People didn't understand the connection between an unborn child and its parent. How many people had told him he could always have more children? Although it was true, he'd never have the child he lost that day in the wreck.

He shook his head. It was stupid to still think that way, but sometimes feelings got in the way of rationality. Something he learned the hard way.

The door opened. "Oh, sorry," his mother whispered.

"No, it's okay. I need to do a few things. You should stay with her." Eric slipped his arm from around Lisa's shoulders and tucked the covers in around her. Her angelic face still looked pale, but she'd stopped shivering, so that was a good sign.

He eyed her blood pressure monitor, which had remained steady since she'd gone to sleep. "She's resting peacefully for now."

"I'm so proud of you, son. I know how difficult this is for you. The look on your face when Lisa went down, it broke my heart. I'm sorry you're reliving this. I'm sorry I got you involved. I never meant—"

"It's okay," he said, laying a hand on his mother's shoulder. "I know your heart's in the right place. But I have to admit, I'm not ready to take on a woman with a baby right now. I just can't." Eric hugged his mother. "Does that make me a horrible person?"

"No. It makes you human." She stepped back and rubbed his arms.

"Besides, there's a father out there. He's just in shock. I'm sure he'll come around. Despite what you say, if a man with that much money made a trip down here, without sending his lawyer, then he must care, right?" He patted her shoulder again and stepped around her. "I'll talk to him."

His mother tightened her grip on his arm. "Eric, you don't know why he's here. You're jumping to conclusions. That man didn't send his lawyer because he probably didn't want anyone to know his real intentions. He wanted Lisa to terminate her babies and wouldn't take no for an answer. She had no choice but to flee New York to escape him. He had her fired from her job, threatened to kill the baby himself if she didn't have an abortion."

Eric's fists tightened at his side, his mother's words clawing at his soul, ripping his insides to pieces. "What?" He looked back at Lisa's sleeping face. "That Son-of-a-bitch. I'd like to take a swing at him, but that won't help Lisa."

"No, it won't, or I would've done it myself already." A blaze of hatred shone in his mother's eyes, like he'd never seen before. Well, once, when some older kid had threatened Eric in fourth grade. He thought she was going to punch the kid's mother.

"Listen, I know you're close to Lisa," he said, "but you can't get in the way. If Mark and her work things out, you have to let her go." His throat tightened with his own words.

"Can you let her go?" his mother asked.

He didn't answer, just released her grip on his arm

and headed for the door. "I'm going to find Mark. We're going to have a little chat. Then I'm sure everything will be how it should. No man would abandon his child, even if he doesn't have feelings for Lisa." He glanced back at the beautiful sleeping angel in the hospital bed behind him and couldn't imagine anyone not loving her kind spirit, strong will, and intelligent mind. She was perfect.

With a deep breath, he opened the door and went in search of Mark who, he was told, had been escorted down to the main floor lobby.

Mark stood at the registration desk, pointing a finger at the poor woman behind the counter. "I'll sue this hospital," he shouted, "the police department and all medical staff. That baby's deformed and not meant to be born. I'm the father and have the right to make that choice."

"Actually, you don't." Eric broke through the crowd that had congregated to watch the show. Sheriff Mason stood by, radioing for backup. This was about to get ugly.

"Mr. Brenson, I'm an attorney of family law and I can assure you the mother has the ultimate decision on the pregnancy." Eric moved closer and continued in a harsh whisper, "And I'd caution you, sir, to be careful what you shout in the waiting room of a small town hospital. They're not too open-minded about abortion around here." Eric nudged him from the registration desk. "Let's speak somewhere a little more private."

"I can say what I want, where I want." Mark's eyes darted to the crowd then back at Eric.

"Mr. Brenson, you might want to reconsider, or I'll be forced to take you into custody for disturbing the peace." Sheriff Mason pointed at the front sliding doors where three more police officers stood waiting for orders.

"I'm sure you'd prefer not to have anything unpleasant reach the newspapers. Even our small local paper might get noticed by someone in New York. You wouldn't want your business associates seeing you on the front page, now would you?" Eric cautioned him, knowing that image was everything in New York.

Mark straightened his suit coat. "You'll be hearing from my attorney," he snapped before marching from the hospital, unwilling to speak to any of them.

Sheriff Mason shrugged. "That man isn't who I'd picture Ms. Mortan with."

Eric had to agree. He retrieved his phone and scrolled through his list of contacts, selecting the one man he trusted from his life in New York. His thumb pressed *call* and he listened to the phone ring, keeping his eyes on Mark through the hospital's glass doors.

"Hey, Eric! How are you?" The deep voice of his former colleague, turned partner, reached from his old life into his current one, something he thought he'd never allow.

"I'm good, Ferris. How are things at the office?" Eric asked.

"Good. It's great seeing *Ferris Walker* on the door. Yep, I made full partner," he announced before Eric could even ask. "I would've never beat you out, so thanks for leaving, man. I owe you one."

"Well, if you mean that, I'd like to collect."

"Oh, sounds serious. You in some kind of legal trouble?"

Eric chuckled. "No, man. I'm looking for information on someone from New York City. A Mark Brenson. I want to know everything you can dig up on him. He's causing some waves down here, and I want to know what his intensions truly are."

"Mark Brenson? Sure, man. I'll have Betty get right on it."

"Good, she's one of the best. Get back to me as soon as you can. It's kind of time sensitive," Eric nudged.

"Okay, you got it. I'll get back to you soon." Ferris terminated the call and Eric lowered to a chair in the waiting room, rubbing his head.

"You okay, darling?" Cathy asked, settling into the chair next to him.

"Yeah, I'm good," Eric lied.

"Sure ya are," she said sarcastically. "It's off the record, you know. Gossip's on vacation at the moment, so why don't you tell me what's going on?"

Eric sighed. "Well, I got a buddy of mine in New York checking out Mr. Brenson.

"Good. That's fantastic. I don't like that smug son of a gun. He's hurt our Lisa, and we don't take kindly to strangers hurting our friends and neighbors."

"Is she, though? Is she part of our town? Or does she belong with Mr. Brenson?

"Do you think that sweet girl in there deserves that monster?" Cathy shrieked.

"It's not my place to decide that," Eric mumbled.

"Then what do you hope to find out from your friend in New York?" Cathy quirked her head, daring him to lie to her again.

Eric sighed. "That's the problem. I don't know. If he turns out to be some rich guy who just got scared then they can work things out."

"Yes, but that's not what you're hoping for," she accused.

"It's what would be easiest." Eric clasped his hands together and lowered his head.

"Sometimes greatness doesn't come from easy. It comes from the heart, and I've seen the way you look at Lisa. That's greatness."

His chest tightened and he rubbed it to relieve the constricting turmoil of his heart.

CHAPTER TWENTY-FIVE

Lisa's eyes fluttered opened. Golden light filtered in through the blinds, a few scattered rays falling on Eric's face as he slouched in the reclining chair, sleeping, his neck cocked awkwardly to the side. Poor man looked uncomfortable.

She clucked her tongue against the thick film coating the roof of her mouth, but found no relief. It was as if she'd been eating cotton balls mixed with peanut butter in the middle of a desert. Scooting into a sitting position, she reached for the pitcher of water resting on the tray beside her bed.

Eric shot up. "What do you need? I can get it." The poor man was standing before he'd fully woken up, causing him to stumble. Dark circles lined his eyes and his once immaculate suit was wrinkled, but he still looked amazing with a just-rolled-out-of-bed look.

"I'm fine. I just needed water," she said, the dryness on her tongue making it challenging to speak.

He poured water into a plastic cup and slipped a hand behind her neck to help her sit up. "Here. It should still be cool. I refreshed it an hour or so ago."

She sipped the icy liquid heaven, quenching her thirst. "Thank you."

Leaning her back, he returned the cup to the tray, an awkward silence filling the room.

"You stayed here all night?" she asked.

He nodded.

"I...I don't know what to say." Her mind swirled, trying to think of the last time someone stayed by her side all night, or even an hour for that matter. All she could come up with was a memory from when she was five and had the chicken pox, before her mom had run off.

"Are you up to talk, or are you too tired?" Eric rubbed his forehead and she knew something troubled him. He was a good man, probably wanted to let her down easy. She believed he'd always be kind, but this was too much for any man.

"Yes, but you don't need to say anything. I appreciate your support, but you can go. You didn't ask for this, and it's my problem to deal with." Her voice quivered, betraying her desire to sound strong.

"You misunderstand." Eric spun on the heel of his shiny dress shoes and ran his hand through his hair as he walked around the bed. "I know your secret, but you don't know mine."

She longed to take his hand and tell him there was nothing he could have possibly done that would ever cause her to see him differently, but it was obvious he needed to share. "I'm listening," she said.

"Where to begin..." He returned to the recliner in

the corner of the room and leaned his elbows on his legs. "I grew up in an amazing home, but for some reason it wasn't enough for me. My father and I used to argue all the time about my dreams for the future and what he wanted for me. He'd been a small town man and I wanted a big city life." He shook his head. "If I would've realized back then how much I had and how little money truly meant."

He ran his palm down his stubbly face. "He only wanted me to be happy, I know that now. But when other kids were out playing sport, I stayed home studying. I worked so hard I ended up at the top of my graduating class. I thought that would make him proud. But the day of my graduation, we had our worst argument ever."

Lisa turned on her side to face him, ignoring the IV cords straining around the bed rail. "Any parent would be proud of a child who'd achieved so much," she said.

"Not when it was at the expense of everything else." Eric shoved from the chair and began pacing the room.

Lisa searched for the right words, to say what he needed to hear, but she didn't understand what he was so upset about so she stayed silent.

"You see," he continued, "I wanted to leave Sweetwater County more than anything. I felt suffocated in this small town and I managed to gain entrance into an Ivy League school. But my father couldn't afford it, and wanted to pay to send me to a college closer to home. He said taking out all those student loans would be a huge mistake. I didn't listen, and when I graduated and my loans came due, I had to work to pay them off."

"I had a ton of student loans, too," Lisa offered, unsure of what else to say.

Eric nodded and continued pacing. "Well, that meant there was no small town practice in my future, which broke a few promises I had made." He stopped and put his hands on his hips, sucking in a long deep breath. "There was a girl, Mary Lynn. We had it bad for each other all through high school, and she supported my decision to go away to college. Even when I told her about not returning to Sweetwater after I finished school she stood by my side."

"She sounds like an amazing girl." A twinge of jealousy pinched Lisa's chest, but she wanted to be happy for him. This was the type of girl he deserved.

"Yes. She was."

"Was?" Lisa whispered. Eric paced around her bed once more, but she snatched his hand and tugged him down next to her. "It's okay. You can tell me."

He took another long breath. "I was so wrapped up with work in New York City. The job was demanding and the hours were long. I'd go home on Christmas and other holidays to see her and the family, but for the most part, I just worked. I wanted to wait until I made partner at the firm before we married, but I knew she wanted to be with me, so I told her to pack her things and move in with me. But I was never home." He paused, rubbing his thumb over Lisa's hand. "I worked so much that I didn't notice how unhappy she'd become. Depressed. That was the word she used. One night, I returned home from an exceptionally long day. I'd lost a big client." He shook his head.

Lisa held tight to his hand with both of hers, hoping to provide comfort.

"We had words," Eric continued. "She packed up and headed back to Sweetwater." His voice cracked and he took a stuttered breath. "She didn't tell me." His jaw tightened.

Lisa stroked his arm, fearing the worst. "What didn't she tell you?"

His eyes glazed over, as though he'd traveled back to a time of darkness. "She..." He cleared his throat and tried again. "She never made it back to Sweetwater. A drunk driver ran a red light and struck her car." His hands shook. "I made it to the scene of the accident just before she passed. She died in my arms, right after she told me she was pregnant with our child."

Tears flowed down his cheeks and she brushed them away, but he let go of her hands and stood. "I'm so sorry," she whispered.

"The baby died, too. My child. The doctors confirmed she was three months pregnant." He rubbed his forehead. "Three months and I didn't know. She'd tried to give me a Christmas present that night, a baby rattle, but I was too busy. She never gave it to me. Instead I opened it days after her death."

"It wasn't your fault. It was an accident."

"Perhaps, but I still missed my chance, my chance to do the right thing." He turned and looked at her, his eyes still brimming with unshed tears. "Lisa, you and that man are having a child. Right now he is at his worst, but give him time. He's mourning the loss of one baby and doesn't know what to do about the other. He'll come around."

She stared at him, dumbfounded.

"I know I told you that I wouldn't leave no matter what you told me, but I'm not the father. I can't get in the way of a man and his child. I'll always be around if you need me, but you need to work things out with the father."

"No, it's not like—"

Eric held up his hand. "Trust me, I work these types of cases every day. Men freak out when they first realize they're going to be a father and then they get their heads on straight. He'll be back. Don't worry. No man could ever abandon their child." He scooped his coat off the back of the recliner and turned toward the door. "It's time for me to leave. This baby isn't mine and I don't deserve another chance."

CHAPTER TWENTY-SIX

"Hey, Betty. What did you find out?" Eric spoke into the speaker of his Blue-tooth headset as he drove back to his office.

"The man had a rough beginning," Betty said. "The documents state he was put in foster care because of abandonment. Never really found a home, but ended up fighting his way up the social and economic food chain. He started out in real estate in his hometown, bought some homes near where he grew up, which he sold on loan to friends and neighbors. Based on the article I read, he foreclosed on all of them, putting them out on the street, and sold the land for profit to a septic business. Put quite a few companies in town out of business, too."

"No one is that evil." He turned the corner and headed up a side street. "Why would he do something like that?"

"It was his mother's home town," Betty said. "Apparently, his mother was a small town woman who, according to his father, trapped him into marriage with a baby. The scandal ruined the man's reputation. Back then, you didn't get busted with a baby like that. Based on police records, Mark's father killed himself when he was only ten. The father left a suicide note, stating that Mark's mother ruined his life by trapping him into marrying her. Mark ran away from home, and his mother ended up dying of a drug overdose. After that, he bounced from one foster home to another for the rest of his youth."

"Geesh, that man has to have issues." Eric rolled into the parking lot outside his office and killed the engine.

Betty cleared her throat. "Listen, there's some other stuff I ran across in his background check, which isn't business related."

"What's that?" Eric wrapped his fingers around the leather handle of his briefcase and opened his car door.

"Well, I stumbled upon a few custody suits. He's been accused on a number of occasions of getting women pregnant then leaving them, though most of the women recanted their statements later on. Some appeared to have gotten a lump sum of money while others just disappeared. None of them had children, though. Not that I found."

A sting shot over Eric's flesh. He slammed the car door and marched to his office. "What do you mean, *disappeared*?"

"I'm not sure. It doesn't look like foul play or anything like that. There were no missing person reports or charges filed. Their credit history and job history just ended. I'm thinking they relocated, took on an alias, probably with the help of Mr. Brenson."

"I see. So, the man bullies the girls into either

giving the baby up or having an abortion then relocates them away from his prestigious life." Eric entered the office, passed Connie without a word and tossed his briefcase on his desk. "Thanks, Betty. I appreciate your efforts."

"I don't mind at all. I still owed you for the promotion you put me in for before you left. But don't you have a law practice in your home town?" Betty asked.

"Yes, but it's a small town. I didn't want word getting out about this guy. Thanks again, and as for the promotion, you don't owe me. You earned it. Take care," Eric said before ending the call and placing the phone on top of his briefcase.

"Sir, everything okay?" Connie asked, remaining in the doorway, her laptop in hand.

"Yes." Eric raked his hand through his hair. *Don't do it. This isn't your business.*

"Sir?" Connie stepped into the room. "You look like you just found out your mother's in the hospital."

"Not my mother, but someone I know." Visions of Lisa lying in that bed while that man paced outside her room, urging her to end her baby's life, shredded his resolve. "Can you pull up every previous case in the last ten years regarding child custody prior to birth?"

She nodded and retreated to her desk.

Eric knew the law, but he'd hoped to find some sort of loop hole. If this man didn't want the baby, perhaps Eric could find something to dangle in front of him.

He rolled up his sleeves and sat down just as his

phone buzzed. "Hey, Mom. How's Lisa? Everything okay?"

"Yes, it's you I'm worried about."

"Don't be. Listen, I have to go. I've got a lot of work to do." Eric held the phone to his ear with his shoulder as he retrieved his laptop from his briefcase.

"You do?"

"Yes. I know Lisa's not my client, but I'm doing a little research."

"I knew you couldn't turn your back on her," his mother said with an air of pride in her voice.

"Yes, well, you were right. I couldn't save my child, but maybe I can save Lisa's." Eric cleared his throat, not wanting to talk anymore on the subject.

"You'll let me know if there's anything I can do?" she asked.

"Of course, but for now, keep an eye on Lisa. I'm better off helping her from my desk than the hospital room, but you can't tell her anything. I don't want to get her hopes up."

"Understood. Good luck, son." His mother ended the call and he set his phone on the desk.

"I've got my laptop running a search. You need anything else?" Connie asked.

"No, but I hope you don't mind working some over time. I'll pay you, of course." He opened his laptop and switched it on.

"Not necessary. My cousin Cathy told me about this SOB. I'll work pro bono, too."

"Does everyone know?" Eric asked.

"Pretty much. The entire town's pulling for you to

save the day." She winked.

"I'm not her knight in shining armor, you know. At most, I'm riding a broken down horse cross-country in a snow storm. You know this is a worthless search as much as I do."

"Yet, I know you'll figure something out. You're a big shot corporate attorney from New York City. If nothing else, you're used to bluffing and getting things done."

"Bluffing?" Eric asked, his fingers stopping in the middle of typing in his password.

"Yes." Connie quirked an eyebrow at him.

Eric shot out of his chair. "You're a genius. Put some coffee on, we've got some paperwork to file."

Adam was right. Everyone had their price, something for which they were willing to get their hands dirty. That innocent baby and Lisa was his.

CHAPTER TWENTY-SEVEN

Lisa woke to the sound of the garbage truck taking away her trash. Too bad it couldn't take away her pain. She rolled on her side, her cheeks crusted with dried up tears. Glancing at her clock, she turned off the alarm before it could ring. Seven in the morning, only an hour until she had to be at the hospital for the sonogram and blood work.

Night after night, she'd dreamt of holding her little one in her arms, only to discover its lifeless body wrapped in white cloth. A shiver shot through her and she folded into herself. Daytime was no better, filled with the knowledge she'd lost one baby already...and Eric.

Her phone chirped, indicating Judy was trying once again to reach her. The woman had been a gem, bringing her food and watching over her without hovering.

I'll be there soon, Judy's text read.

She hadn't told Judy about today's appointment, but it didn't surprise her. Judy had a way of finding things out.

No need. I'll come by the antique store after, Lisa replied.

She had to be strong and figure this out on her own. Just like she'd always done. It was time to stop depending on Judy. She was Eric's family, not Lisa's.

Lisa pushed from the bed and dressed slowly, reminding herself that she had to follow the doctor's instructions to the letter, avoiding stress, getting lots of rest, eating and drinking properly, and taking her vitamins. She'd never been sedentary for so long. It had been torture.

After brushing her teeth, she slid on her tennis shoes, not wanting to risk a fall on the icy sidewalks, and retrieved her coat.

Ding Dong.

Lisa traipsed to the door and peeked through the side window. Judy stood on her front porch, waving back at her. "It's just me. Open up. It's cold."

Lisa swung the door open. "What are you doing here?"

"Oh, hon. You didn't really think I'd let you travel to the hospital on your own, did you?"

Lisa shook her head. "It's only five miles from here."

"Doesn't matter, I want to be there with you. Besides, you're on bed rest. So, I'll drive." Judy about-faced and marched from Lisa's little rented house, brooking no further discussion.

A bitter chill swept up the front walk. Lisa hesitated, wanting to return to the warmth and safety of her bed. Yes, it had been torture lying still for so long, but anything was better than facing potentially bad news of her baby.

"Come on, now," Judy called from the car.

Lisa locked the front door and shuffled to the car, avoiding icy patches. As she climbed into the passenger seat, a warm air blowing from the vents and Judy's Lilac perfume greeted her. A scent she'd grown fond of.

Judy slid the car into gear then guided it down the drive and onto the quaint side street before turning onto Main. A soft tune about love and loss sang from the speaker by Lisa's leg, an appropriate cadence for her ride to the hospital.

In an attempt to force her racing thoughts toward something positive, she slid her finger up to illuminate the display on her phone and glanced over her email.

"You haven't heard from him at all?" Judy asked.

Lisa scrolled through the messages. "I wasn't checking for that. I thought I might have some business to take care of."

Judy patted Lisa's hand. "Hon, you know you can't lie to me."

Lisa bowed her head. "No, not a word. How did you know?"

"I know you. And besides, the online shop isn't even active yet, so what business would there be?"

Lisa straightened in her seat. "I meant to tell you about that. It's just with everything that happened. I mean, I'd never start something without speaking to you first. How did you find out about it?"

"Calm down. I knew you wouldn't do anything without speaking to me. Cathy mentioned it. She stopped in the other day and asked about it. Of course, it was an excuse to find out how you're doing. And, of course, she wanted to gossip and speculate about what happened before you arrived here."

Lisa chuckled. "In her own way, I think she cares."

"Oh, she cares all right. She's got a big heart, but she has a mouth to match it. Don't get me wrong, I love Cathy. She was there for me a long time ago. It's just, I've learned to keep some things to myself. Everyone in the town has a big heart. We're just all different in how we show it."

Judy rolled to a stop and lowered her window while guiding the car into the parking garage. The loud buzz from the ticket machine erupted until Judy snatched the gold paper and drove forward, pulling into a space on the second aisle.

Every moment that ticked away, Lisa willed the news to be good. "Judy?"

"Yes?"

"Thank you," Lisa mumbled, twisting her purse strap.

"For what, honey?"

"Being here. Everyone always leaves me. But the one person that should turn her back to be with her son is by my side."

Judy leaned over and wrapped her arms around Lisa. "Oh, hon. I know you worry about being alone, but you don't have to. I'm going to be here through the entire pregnancy."

"No." Lisa leaned back, her heart turning into a solid mass. "If the baby's okay then I'm leaving. I'll go back to New York and face the music. I'll figure out how to deal with Mark, but it's time for me to stand on my own two feet." The words she'd practice sounded robotic, even to her, but she had to do this. It wasn't fair to separate a mother and son because of her issues. "And if the baby's not okay, well, then..."

"Shh. Enough of this non-sense," Judy scolded. "Now, first of all, my son would want you to stay, so don't go leaving because you think it's better for him. It's not. I'm his mother and you're what's good for him. He just doesn't know it yet. He's scared. After losing one woman and baby, he can't bring himself to face that kind of loss again. Not yet. Yes, he did step aside, thinking Mark should be the one here for you, but if he knew Mark wasn't here—"

"You can't tell him that. I won't have him around because he feels sorry for me."

Judy held up one hand. "I don't break my promises. But, I think you're both being silly. As for the health of the baby, I'm sure everything's fine. Now, get over yourself and get your tail end out of this car and into that office."

Lisa unbuckled and opened the car door. She knew better than to argue with Judy. If Eric hadn't won an argument with her, Lisa didn't stand a chance. Lisa climbed out of the car and followed Judy to the lobby.

The woman had to be an angel and Lisa couldn't bear to hurt her. Judy put on a brave face, but Lisa knew that losing her one true love all those years ago had destroyed her. Only Eric had filled a void in Judy's heart, and Lisa couldn't take that away. No, even if she had to leave in the middle of the night she would, but she refused to be in the way of Judy and her son. He'd been 'out of town' on business since that day in hospital, but Lisa knew he didn't want to return because of her.

The elevator ride to the diagnostic wing dragged on, stopping with a ding on every floor, until they reached five. Entering the office, a few people already waited in the stiff armchairs. The sight of magazines, the smell of disinfectant, and the murmured conversations around the front desk made her heart race.

Judy directed her to one of the chairs. "Sit before you fall down. I'll sign you in."

Lisa lowered into a chair and listened to Judy ramble off questions for twenty minutes as she filled out the form. Finally, Judy placed the pen on the clipboard and leaned toward her. "For a girl who didn't want to be pregnant and thought she'd make a bad mother, you sure do look petrified about facing the possibility of not being pregnant. I think you have your answer. You were born to be a mother. Trust me, I'm always right. Just ask Eric."

Lisa and Judy sat in silence, Lisa going over all the possibilities in her head. She'd been researching every known deformity and disorder she could think of on the internet. If the child had autism, she'd have a difficult time, but would face the challenge to the best of her ability. For a missing limb, there was always therapy. Even a more severe disorder didn't stop her from wanting the baby. She just prayed it was still alive in there. She'd willed it to move in her womb, growing anxious when she didn't feel anything for long periods of time, but the most she'd ever felt was the butterfly movement in her belly.

"Lisa Mortan?" a woman dressed in scrubs called from the doorway to the exam rooms.

Lisa trembled.

Judy took her hand. "Come on, dear."

They followed the narrow white hall to a room, the world sounding as if it came through a tunnel. Staff spoke to her, but Judy answered all their questions. Lisa only focused on the health of the baby.

Judy's phone, vibrating in her purse, ripped Lisa from her blank state, but Judy ignored it. When the nurse left and Lisa was dressed in her gown and lying on the exam table, Judy's phone vibrated once more.

"Popular woman," Lisa teased, trying to ease her nerves.

Judy smiled. "Not me, darling. It's all questions about you."

"Oh." But who else knew she was getting the sonogram this morning? She hadn't even told Judy about it. "Who?"

"You sure you want to know?" Judy winked.

Lisa's heart fluttered, the only emotion besides terror that had broken through her numbness since she'd woken. "Who?" *It's not him. Don't go there.*

"Eric. He's been texting every five minutes, wanting to know how you're doing. He asked me if Mark was here. But I told him that I didn't think it was my place to tell him, but he's worried about you."

Then he should be here. She shook her head. *No, that's not fair.* He didn't deserve that.

The ultrasound tech came in and Lisa prepared herself for gasps of horror as they looked at her baby.

"Relax, sweetheart. This won't hurt. Okay, let's take a look and listen for the baby's heartbeat." The nurse turned the monitor so they could all see. An image of a head appeared on screen, but quickly whirled away. The woman kept swishing back and forth, but only paused for a second then moved on.

"Is everything okay?" Lisa asked.

"Yes, dear." The tech clicked a few more buttons on the ultrasound machine then stood up. "Stay right here, Ms. Mortan. I'll be right back."

"There's something wrong? You couldn't find a heartbeat, could you?" Lisa started trembling, her body shaking like she'd never imagined it could.

"You need to calm down. I'll be right back." The tech's eyes were wide with fear as she fled the room.

"Oh, God. I knew I didn't deserve to be a mom."

Judy's eyes were brimming with tears, but she took Lisa's hand. "Now, you stop that. We don't know anything yet."

The door opened once more and Dr. Hendricks came in with another woman dressed in scrubs. "Ms. Mortan. How are you today? Are you cold?"

Lisa could only shake her head as her body continued to tremble.

"Nurse Thompson, please get some heated blankets for Ms. Mortan," he said, then turned back to Lisa. "I need you to calm down and listen to me. The nurse was unable to locate the heartbeat, but I have the best tech in the hospital right here, Ms. Janson. We spoke about the possibilities of the remaining fetus. Now, I need you to be brave so that she can check. Can you do that for me?"

Lisa's teeth chattered so loud she barely heard Judy's phone buzzing again. Judy ignored it and clutched Lisa's hand. Holding onto Judy tight, Lisa nodded.

The tech sat down. "I'm going to turn the volume all the way up and I'll be pushing on you a little here and there. Is that okay?"

Lisa nodded again. She fought the shaking and tried to be still, but her belly rolled inside out and she clutched her middle. "Oh."

Ms. Janson smiled. She only touched Lisa for a second before a loud pounding sound echoed in the room. "Ah, I think we've found your baby."

Tears streamed down Lisa's face. Nurse Thompson returned and warm blankets wrapped around her shoulders and feet. Judy squeezed her hand. People spoke, but no words reached her ears. Only the beautiful, loud thumping of her baby' heart filled her ears.

After several minutes, during which Ms. Janson took measurements, Dr. Hendricks turned to Lisa and shook her hand. "You had me worried for a minute. I thought you were going to go into shock, breaking my perfect record of never losing a patient to emotional distress."

Judy and the nurses all chuckled along with him

while Lisa stared at the ceiling, listening to her baby's heartbeat.

"Ms. Janson, can you please show Ms. Mortan to my office when she's ready?" Dr. Hendricks said.

"Certainly, Doctor," Ms. Janson agreed, then handed Lisa a picture of her baby.

The entire time Lisa dressed, all she could do was stare at the picture in disbelief. No matter what came next, she could handle it.

Ms. Janson led her to Dr. Hendricks' office, Judy by her side the whole way. When they reached the small room, Judy pulled out her cell. "Oh, my. I think I freaked Eric out. Poor kid. It's killing him not to be here."

Lisa didn't respond. She sat in one of the office chairs, staring at her baby's picture, her heart full of love and hope for the first time since she could remember.

Dr. Hendricks entered and sat down behind the hard wood desk. "Well, Ms. Mortan. I must say you've been my most interesting and exciting case. Congratulations."

"Thank you," Lisa said.

Dr. Hendricks' expression turned serious. "But I'm afraid this is one of those pregnancies where the drama won't end until the baby is born. You see, the baby is small, and there is Echogenic Foci on the heart. There's a chance the baby could have down syndrome or another disorder."

"How do we find out?" Judy asked.

"There are two options. You can have an

amniocentesis—"

"You said that was too dangerous," Lisa quipped.

"I still believe that," Dr. Hendricks said, "but ultimately, it's your decision. The chances of preterm labor are high."

"What's the other option?" Lisa asked.

Dr. Hendricks closed the folder and laid it on the desk in front of him.

CHAPTER TWENTY-EIGHT

Lisa set the sonogram picture next to her laptop and pulled her chair closer to the table. The smell of cinnamon and spice wafted from candles set on the counter and the table in front of her. "It's good to be back at work."

Judy set a cup of warm tea with honey next to Lisa's computer then handed her a throw. "I'm sure, but I promised Dr. Hendricks you'd stay seated as much as possible. No heavy lifting, bending, or excessive stress, got it?"

"Yes, ma'am," Lisa teased. Opening her laptop, she checked for emails or instant messages, a routine she'd started since she left Eric a message, asking to speak with him. Clicking on Skype, she searched for him, but he wasn't logged in."

"He's been out of town," Judy mumbled on her way by.

"Oh." *Still avoiding me, huh?* "Well, maybe someday he'll give me a chance to apologize, but until then, I'm going to concentrate on the health of this baby. I won't take any more chances. If bed rest did anything for me, it was to force me to sit still long enough to face my demons." Her stomach fluttered and she smiled. "I'm not my mother, and it's not all about what I want anymore. It's what this baby needs."

Judy sat down next to her and took a sip of her tea. "You need to be happy, too, though. As I said before, you have choices."

"You mean Eric?" Lisa sighed. "Judy, I love you more than I thought possible, and there isn't anything I want more in this world than to be your daughter, but it's not going to happen. Eric won't even return my calls."

"Yes, but—"

"I know, but it doesn't matter what happened before. I'm not the girl he once knew. He chose to leave because this was all too much for him. I respect that. I'll admit I wanted to check out myself a few times. But it's better for him to leave now, rather than later when I've grown closer to him. Besides, it's best he isn't here until the baby's born." She rubbed her belly. "I'm guessing he struggles with the thought of me losing the baby as much as I do. I'd never want him to face the pain of what happened to him again, especially because of me." She fought the sadness in her heart, the deep, I'll-never-find-love-again kind of stabbing pain she'd fought so hard to ignore, but couldn't. Instead, she repeated her new mantra in her head. *It's not about me anymore. It's about the baby.*

"I don't believe he just disappeared." Judy's gaze dropped to her hands, and for the first time Lisa realized this had hurt not only herself, but Judy, too.

Lisa reached across the table and gripped her dear friend's hand. "I know he left town, and I hope I'm not the cause of it. But I'll leave tomorrow if you think it will help your son return." Lisa fought to say it, prayed Judy wouldn't agree, but she knew she'd do anything for the woman at her side.

"No, dear. If Eric left because of this, then he wasn't ready to return to Sweetwater to begin with. I'd thought that from the beginning, but he wouldn't hear it. No, I think he's fighting with his own demons, and I truly don't think you leaving will bring him home. Besides, I couldn't part with you." She looked at Lisa with glistening eyes. "After all, I'm gonna be a grandma."

"Judy..." Lisa struggled to keep the tears at bay, but she couldn't help embracing the woman who had shown her more compassion than anyone else in her life. "You're the most amazing woman I've ever met."

Judy sat back, still holding on to both of Lisa's hands. "Oh, dear, you need to get out more."

Lisa smiled. "There's something I'd like to do, for closure, but I wanted to ask you if it's okay."

"What's that, dear?" Judy asked.

"I'd like to send Eric an apology email. It's time to let go and move on. I can't sit here waiting for him to walk through the door for the rest of my life."

Judy nodded. "If anyone understands how that feels, it's me." She scooted her chair back and collected their teacups. "I'll warm these up."

Taking a deep cleansing breath, Lisa clicked on

compose message and started typing.

Dear Eric,

I understand why you left Sweetwater County and I'll respect your decision not to speak to me, but I still wanted to apologize. Despite our promise to keep our secrets from each other until you returned, I should have insisted on telling you the truth. It's not an excuse, but you were my one ray of light during weeks of darkness. Each day, all I could think about was coming home in time to see your face on Skype and talk to you for hours. It was selfish, and I'm truly sorry.

For a minute, part of me thought you could play father to my unborn child and I could leave all the ugliness of a man, who changed overnight from sweet to sadistic, behind in New York, but now I know it was just a fantasy. I'm sorry I got you caught up in all this craziness.

I had to try one last time to reach you and promise that if you're willing to return to Sweetwater County, I'll leave immediately. Judy's the most amazing woman, and the thought of coming between you and your mother is breaking my heart. Please, with one word from you, I'll go and you'll never have to see me again.

Sincerely,

Lisa

She placed her finger over the *enter* button, but hesitated. If she sent this, she'd have to follow through if he wanted her gone. Yet, leaving would be the hardest thing she'd ever have to do. What would happen to the business? How would she raise the baby on her own? Was she ready to leave, to stand on her own two feet with no help?

Yes, she'd done it her entire life.

She pressed *enter* then sat back in the tall wicker chair. Her hands still shook, so she took several more deep breaths, trying to calm herself. Avoiding stress was too important. It was in Eric's hands now. Judy had been too kind to her to keep the mother from her son.

The front door swung open and Cathy Mitchell filed into the store, with a few other people and Sheriff Mason in tow.

Lisa scooted her chair back then stood. "What's going on?"

Cathy shooed her back into her seat then stood behind her. "Nothing to worry about, darling. Your town family has you covered."

"What?" Lisa asked.

Wanda, the woman who'd bought the candlesticks, came to stand beside her. "That's right, dear."

Judy exited the kitchen. "Jimmy, nice to see you here. Thanks for the heads up."

Lisa swiveled back and forth, looking to each person for answers. "I don't understand. What's going on?"

"Honey, I know you don't know much about having a family, but you've got one now," Wanda said. Lisa gaped at her. "Oh, don't look surprised. You should know already that Mrs. Gossip, Cathy Mitchell, told the entire town all about your past and what's been going on. Well, we don't take kindly to strangers in our town."

"I'm technically a stranger," Lisa mumbled.

"Hush with that nonsense. You're one of us now," Cathy scolded.

The door swung open with a bang and Mark stood in the entryway covered in muddy water. "You people are insane."

"Oh, did my car spray you when I passed? I'm truly sorry." Cathy sounded sincere, but her curled lip spoke volumes of mischievous joy.

"Sheriff, I'd like to report my car being stolen." Mark eyed the five women surrounding Lisa. She didn't even know all their names, but it didn't matter. They stood in her defense.

"Really? We haven't had a car theft since 2004, when Mr. Williams forgot he gave his wife the keys to the car. Of course, Mr. Williams forgets a lot of things."

They all nodded and smiled while Lisa tried to keep up with everything that was going on. Her neck ached from trying to follow the banter.

Sheriff pulled a leather bound flip pad from a pouch on his belt. "What kind of car is it?"

"A BMW. It's a rental, so I don't know the plates."

"I remember something about a fancy pants car," the sheriff said. "Hmm...let me see." He flipped through several pages. "Ah, here it is. You can pick that up at Chuck's Impound Lot at the edge of town. It was illegally parked, so the owner of a store had it towed."

"Illegally parked? There wasn't a sign."

"Really? Well, if you'd like to dispute it, you can take the ticket to Sarah, my wife. She's the town judge. I'm sure she can clear this up."

Mark's face turned a shade of crimson Lisa had never seen before. He glared at her. "We need to talk."

Cathy slid a hand over one shoulder, while Wanda did the same on the other side and Lisa's shoulders warmed from the touch. Judy walked to the side of the table and smiled. "We're here with you, dear."

Lisa smiled back at her then lifted her chin. "Then talk," she told him.

"Figures you can't fight your battles on your own. You never belonged in my world."

"Thank you. That's the best compliment you've ever given me. As you can see, I don't have to fight my battles alone anymore, and since when is a beautiful unborn baby a battle? I'm happy, Mark. For the first time in my life, I've found a place I truly belong, and I'm happy. I've told you a million times that you'll never have to see me again. I'll have this baby on my own."

"You're darn right you won't see me again. Right after I see the results of a paternity test." He slid a packet of paperwork from his inner coat pocket and dropped it on the table. "My lawyer filed to demand the paternity test. If it's mine, then I'll sue for sole custody."

Lisa gasped, her hands protectively surrounding her belly. "You don't even want the baby. Now you're going to raise it?"

"I won't, but that doesn't matter. If I take the baby

from you, then I'll never have to worry about you changing your mind and suing me for all I've got."

"That's all you care about, isn't it? Your money." She clenched her fist on the table. "This is a life. My baby's life. You'd seriously fight me for custody?"

"Absolutely." Mark's set jaw told her he wasn't bluffing. He'd do anything to rid his life of a pregnant woman.

Her mind swirled with options. How could she save her child from this man?

"It's not yours," she blurted. Lisa lowered her head. She didn't want to look Judy straight in the eyes. They'd probably all walk out the door, thinking she really was the slut Mark claimed her to be, but what else could she do? "You were right. I had an affair. I only wanted to sue you for the money, but now I can see it was a horrible idea. There's no reason to have a paternity test. The baby isn't yours. I'm sorry." Lisa kept her head down, fighting the sting of tears.

"You're just telling me that so I'll leave," Mark sneered. "Too bad. We're going to finish this. You wanted to sue me, then sue me. You know I'll win. I've got the best lawyers in the country. No matter what though," Mark stepped closer and rested his knuckles on the other end of the table, "you'll never hold that baby in your arms."

Lisa stared at him in horror as a few gasps escaped the women standing behind her.

"Excuse me."

Lisa turned to see Eric standing in the kitchen doorway.

Judy rushed around the table, but Eric held up one hand, stopping her.

Lisa's pulse thrummed against her throat. What was he doing here?

Eric shuffled forward. "Sheriff, Mom, Cathy, Wanda." He nodded to each then inserted himself between them to face Mark. He stood eye to eye with Mark, each staring down the other.

"Oh!" Lisa's stomach tightened so quickly she couldn't help but yelp.

Sheriff Mason stepped forward. "Now, boys. Ms. Lisa isn't supposed to have any stress. Let's keep things civil."

Eric stepped back and lowered to one knee by Lisa's side. He ran his hand through his hair then touched her arm. "Are you okay?"

Lisa couldn't speak. All she could manage was a nod of her head. She breathed slow and steady until the cramp subsided.

"I got your message, but it wasn't necessary, I'd already made my decision. I just had to work something out first." He shot Mark a sideways glance then looked back at Lisa. "Listen, darling—"

Darling?

"—I know we didn't plan this, and I can't blame you if you hate me for abandoning you, but I'm here now. I guess having an affair turn so serious so quickly frightened me away, but I want to be a father, and I hope you'll have me."

"You? Her?" Mark slammed a fist down on the table then stormed around the room, knocking an antique lamp over. "No. I'm not leaving here without that amnio thing being done."

"It's too risky. I won't do it," Lisa shouted.

Eric took her hand. "I'm here. I won't leave again." He kissed each knuckle, sending hope shooting into her heart, but it was all a ruse, right? This crazy town had convinced him to put on a good show for Mark. That was the only explanation.

Eric stood, lifted his briefcase from the floor, opened it and tossed a folder on top of Mark's paperwork. "This document declares me as the father. It's already signed, notarized, and filed with the county court house. On the day of the birth, my name will be listed on the birth certificate. It doesn't matter if you believe me or not. I'm the father legally."

Mark's nose twitched and he lifted the folder to examine the paperwork inside.

Lisa reached out and grabbed Eric's arm. "You don't have to do this."

"It doesn't matter in ten years, twenty? She can't claim the child is mine?" Mark asked.

"No," Eric said. "You walk out a free man under one condition."

"What's that?"

"You leave this town and never return. You never speak to Lisa or anyone else in this town ever again."

"Sold," Mark said without hesitation, tossing the folder back down on the table. His shoulders relaxed. "Thank God that nightmare's over. You're crazy for taking that whore on."

Eric stepped forward, fisting his hands, his back

tense and arms straining the seams of his jacket.

"It's time you got your car out of the impound lot and were on your way," Sheriff Mason said, guiding him quickly out of the building.

Lisa didn't know what to make of it all, but she knew she needed to tell the truth to the people surrounding her. She couldn't let them think Eric had an affair with some woman in New York City. "Judy, it's not true."

"All I care about is I'm gonna be a grandmama. Nothing else really matters."

"Congratulations, you two," Cathy said. "These kids now days, always doing things backwards. Kids then marriage." She harrumphed as she meandered through the merchandise toward the door, Wanda trailing her.

"You know we've got your back, sister," Wanda called over her shoulder.

"You mean I got her back," Cathy retorted before the door swung shut behind them.

"I need to go run an errand. Can you keep an eye on Lisa for a bit? She's not to move out of that chair." Judy swung her coat around her shoulders. What was it with her always needing to run errands the moment the three of them were alone?

Eric just nodded.

Judy kissed Lisa's cheek. "Have faith, darling," she whispered. The kitchen door swooshed behind her.

Alone with Eric, she held tight to the arm of the chair, trying to figure out what all this meant between them. Was he just doing a good deed, rescuing her from legal troubles because that was his job? "Thank you," she said softly. "You didn't have to do that, but now I can leave without having to worry about him following me."

"Leave? You can't go anywhere." Eric pulled out the chair next to her. "I'm sorry that I left, but I had so much to think about." He squeezed her hand. "I've made so many mistakes in the past and I didn't want to get in the way of someone else's happiness. If there was a chance for Mark and—"

"No chance," Lisa blurted. "There never was."

"Yeah, I see that now." His thumb twirled around her knuckles, soothing her apprehension. "I let Mary Lynn down once, blamed myself for many years for her accident and the death of them both." His voice cracked and she wanted to hug him, to tell him it wasn't his fault.

"You see, it all came flooding back when I saw all the blood..." His voice cracked again. "And then when I heard you'd lost a baby."

Lisa took a stuttered breath. He looked at her, his tear-filled eyes matching her own. "It wasn't your fault."

"I know, but I thought I'd failed again. That I should have stayed here instead of going off to Europe to work. That if I had—"

"It still would have happened. It was my stress, not yours. You had nothing to do with it."

Eric cupped her face. "It wasn't your fault, either. The doctor said it happens, remember? Carrying twins is trickier and sometimes things go wrong."

Tears streamed down her face and her throat closed tight. He brushed the moisture from her cheeks with his thumb. "We've both made plenty of mistakes, and I don't know if we can work everything out, but I can tell you that you captured, not only my attention with your beauty, but my heart. I've never met a woman like you. I know you're special. I sensed how big your heart was the moment I first met you." He rested his forehead against hers. "I'll be here for you and the baby always. If things work out between us, and I hope they do, then we'll have an amazing life together. But even if they don't, I can promise you one thing, Mom and I will still be here for you and that baby no matter what happens."

Lisa fought to control her emotions. "I don't have to leave?"

Eric smiled. "No. You're here to stay. With me, I hope." He slipped his hand onto her belly. "Both of you."

Lisa's lip quivered. "I'd like that."

Eric wrapped his arms around her, lifting her until she stood. He captured her lips and this time she gave into the heartwarming pleasure of his minty taste, musky aroma, and strong arms with all she had. Her entire world spun faster than when she'd been drugged in the hospital, but this time she remained secure in Eric's arms. When he drew back and rested his forehead to hers, she clutched his waist tight.

"It's true then," she whispered.

"What is?" Eric asked.

Lisa smiled, and pressed a chaste kiss to his lips.

"The sign. Sweetwater County really is where hearts and families belong."

He kissed the top of her head and she knew she never wanted to be anywhere else. Ever.

THE END

If you've enjoyed this story please take a second to write a review or tell a friend about what you've read.

A great way to keep up to date on all releases, sales and prizes is to subscribe to Ciara Knight's Newsletter.

Ciara is extremely sociable, so feel free to chat with her on Facebook, Twitter, or Goodreads.

For more information please visit
http://www.ciaraknight.com.
Or send her an email at:
ciara@ciaraknight.com

ABOUT THE AUTHOR

Ciara Knight writes to 'Defy the Dark' with her fantasy and paranormal books.

Her debut novel, **The Curse of Gremdon**, was released to acclaimed reviews, securing a Night Owl Top Pick and five stars from the Paranormal Romance Guild. Also, released in 2012 is her young adult series, *Battle for Souls*. Book I, **Rise From Darkness**, won July Book of the Month at Long and Short Reviews.

Ciara's newest young adult/new adult Amazon best-selling series, *The Neumarian Chronicles*, launched in 2013, causing an "uprising" of attention from fans and reviewers.

When not writing, she enjoys reading all types of fiction. Some great literary influences in her life include Edgar Allen Poe, Shakespeare, Francine Rivers and J K Rowling.

Her first love, besides her family, reading, and writing, is travel. She's backpacked through Europe, visited orphanages in China, and landed in a helicopter on a glacier in Alaska.

Ciara is extremely sociable and can be found at Facebook, Twitter, Goodreads, Pinterest, and her blog.

Made in the USA
San Bernardino, CA
09 March 2016